FASCINATED
THE WICKED WOODLEYS BOOK 6

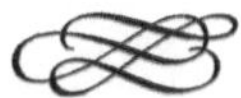

JESS MICHAELS

Fascinated

A Wicked Woodleys Novella

For more information, contact Jess Michaels

www.AuthorJessMichaels.com

To contact the author:

Email: Jess@AuthorJessMichaels.com

Instagram: @JessMichaelsBks

Facebook: www.facebook.com/JessMichaelsBks

Jess Michaels offers exclusive content to newsletter subscribers! Join here: http://www.authorjessmichaels.com/

When I wrote Seduced, I thought it would be the final chapter in the Woodley saga. But the more I got to know Aaron and Griffin, the more I came to realize they belonged together. My thanks goes to Mackenzie Walton and Jenn LeBlanc for giving me the courage to embrace their story the way I wanted to.

Also to Michael, as always. A wise philosopher once said, "love is a battlefield". With you, it has always been worth every fight. Put your back on me.

CHAPTER 1

1827

"Look at all the children!"

Griffin Merrick glanced up from his book with a start as his mother shook his arm with more force than was perhaps necessary. She held back the curtain on the carriage window, and he looked past her to the outside.

He hadn't realized they had already come through the gate at the Woodley country estate outside of Idleridge, but they had somehow weaved their way past the large manor house and down the long hill to where two additional homes had been built years ago. They were not quite as large as the estate home, but still impressive.

Outside of one of them stood Griffin's sister Letty and her husband Jack Blackwood, along with their three children. Everyone was smiling and waving, and Griffin took a deep breath so he could force a smile onto his own face. There was no use bringing the melancholy he'd felt in London out into the country air.

The carriage stopped, but before the footman could climb down to assist, Jack stepped forward to open the carriage door himself.

"Welcome," he said, his smile wide and friendly. He held out his right hand to Mrs. Merrick first, and Griffin winced as Jack's other arm trembled. Jack had been injured almost a decade ago and the use of his left arm remained highly restricted.

A fact that was Griffin's fault. Whenever he saw Jack, it was a reminder of the past he had to overcome, the responsibility he had to take seriously every moment of every day for the rest of his life. He already knew the results of being irresponsible.

"Griffin," Jack said as he handed off Mrs. Merrick so she could rush forward into the arms of screeching, laughing grandchildren, as well as her daughter.

Griffin stepped down from the carriage and was surprised when Jack drew him in for a bear hug strong enough to show the injured arm didn't trouble him much. Griffin didn't know why he was shocked by the action—Jack was never anything but kind and brotherly toward him.

Whether or not he deserved it.

"Come on," Jack said, slinging his right arm around Griffin's shoulders. "The children are anxious to see their uncle."

"They seem very excited," Griffin said cautiously as they approached the lot of them. The youngest, Adam, who was just two, was leaping up and down with glee while the older two, Jillian and James, were both talking at once.

Jack laughed at his boisterous brood. "They are. All the Woodleys arrived earlier today, so there are slightly more than a dozen children up at the big house right now."

"I see," Griffin said, but got to say no more on the subject as his older sister Letty managed to extract herself from her children and mother, and all but floated over to him. She wrapped her arms around him as she pressed a kiss to his cheek.

"Griffin," she said, her eyes bright with pleasure. "I'm so glad you're here. It seems like an age since we've seen you."

Griffin frowned slightly. It *had* been a long time. After their father's death a year prior, he had busied himself with all the details surrounding his inheritance, along with visiting estates and managing investments. That and…*other* things he doubted his sister would approve of.

Perhaps that was the real reason he'd stayed away.

"You look wonderful," he said, and meant it. Letty had blossomed since her marriage to Jack and she looked even more beautiful now than she had as a blushing girl.

She shook her head. "I look like the mother of three very excitable children. Come and see them all, they have been dying to hug you."

As Letty took Jack's hand, the two led him the final few steps to where the children were standing with his mother. There were squeals of welcome and hugs all around, and for the moment Griffin forgot everything except for Jillian, James and Adam.

But soon enough, they migrated into the house, and after some pleading the children were allowed to walk up to the manor on the hill to play with their cousins. Griffin sighed as quiet enveloped the parlor where the adults had settled once again.

"Are War and Claire already up at the big house, then?" Mrs. Merrick asked as Letty poured and prepared tea for everyone.

Jack smiled in answer. "Yes. When the clan arrived, my brother and Claire and their children headed up to be part of the welcome, but we'll join them all for supper."

"And you are here for ten whole days, so you will have plenty of time to catch up with Woodley doings," Letty said as she brought a cup for their mother. "I'm so glad we decided to have this party."

Griffin nodded. Normally he avoided a party at all costs. He only went to balls in London when his mother forced the issue. Even then he tried his level best to sneak out early, much to Mrs. Merrick's chagrin.

"What is the occasion again?" he asked.

Letty and Jack exchanged a laugh and a look that spoke volumes of their love and connection, which had not diminished in the nine years since their marriage. In fact, Griffin would say it had only increased.

"*That* is hard to nail down," Letty explained. "The Woodleys and the Blackwoods are such a big clan, especially after all the marriages and babies, if we are all together it's a party in itself. Someone made the suggestion of inviting others and here we are, a massive country gathering about to happen."

"Who have you invited?" Mrs. Merrick asked.

Letty began to rattle off a few names, many from the connected Flynn clan, and Griffin was about to let his mind wander when she said, "And Aaron Condit, of course."

Griffin swallowed and turned his full attention to his sister. "Mr. Condit will be here?" he repeated, hoping there was no extra interest to his tone.

"Yes," Jack said. "Letty thought he could use some time outside of London."

Letty's face darkened with a shade of concern. "He works too hard."

Griffin nodded slowly. He often thought the same thing of Aaron. The man had been the best friend of Letty's first husband, the Viscount Seagate, and Aaron and Letty had stayed friends themselves since Seagate's untimely death. In fact, Griffin would say Aaron was Letty's *best* friend outside of Jack.

Which made Griffin's life far more complicated. After all, he saw Aaron himself from time to time. In certain clubs. Special clubs meant for men of Griffin's...*inclinations*. The first time he'd seen Aaron in one of those places, his stomach had flipped with pure, unadulterated fear. What if Aaron told his secret?

But then he'd realized that Aaron's appearance there meant he, too, had different urges from the average man in Society. Once it became clear that was true, Griffin had found himself seeking Aaron out in the crowd with increasing frequency. They talked from time to time, never acknowledging the secret they had in common.

And then there had been the one night when Griffin had secretly followed Aaron to a private room at the Wild Boar Club. One of the proprietor's special rooms where observers could…*watch*. And watch he had. Those images still burned in his brain.

"And when will Mr. Condit arrive?" Griffin asked, hearing the strain in his own tone and hoping it wouldn't be questioned.

"Later this afternoon," Letty said.

"In a sea of married people, there shall be at least *two* eligible gentlemen of means," Mrs. Merrick said with a laugh. "The unmatched ladies of the village will be all atwitter at the welcoming ball tomorrow, Griffin. You shall have your pick of ladies between you, I would wager."

Griffin sat stiffly as Letty began to speak to her mother about something to do with young Jillian's proficiency on the pianoforte. He was happy for the distraction, for he had heard the hopefulness in his mother's voice when she spoke of eligible ladies.

She was forever pressuring him to settle down and wed, to produce children as Letty had. Except his children would be heirs and carry on the family name. Very important to her, as it had been important to his late father.

Of course, no one knew how difficult that was going to be for him. He had tried. God knew he had tried. He'd danced with women, he'd chatted with them in ballrooms as he fought desperately to create any attraction within himself. A few times he'd even been so driven as to go to a bawdy house. But nothing worked. He looked at women, the most beautiful and desirable of women, and felt…nothing.

But with men it was different. No matter how he tried to change it or starve it out of himself, that was a fact. A fact that had driven him to try to push away the life his parents had built for him. A fact that had made him reckless. A fact that had nearly gotten Jack and Letty killed.

Once that happened, he had settled into the life his family wanted, but never fully accepted the future. He doubted he would marry. It didn't seem fair to do so and saddle a wife with his lack of interest and fidelity.

Not to mention marrying seemed the best way to ensure his secrets came out. If he could not perform his martial duties, that would ultimately be revealed, and questions would be asked and troubles raised and even arrests made.

He shuddered.

"You still with us?" Jack said, leaning closer to Griffin with a half-smile.

Griffin blinked. "What? Yes, apologies. The ride was long—I suppose I lost myself in thought."

Jack tossed a side glance at the ladies, who now seemed to be discussing hats. He grinned. "Only one of us will escape this, you know. Both of us aren't going to survive. So I'll sacrifice myself for you."

Griffin swallowed hard. "What do you mean?"

"Go for a walk. Get away from the talk of sashes, which is likely to follow the hat...*situation*. I'll make your excuses."

Griffin stared at him. Jack was teasing, but he was also offering him a very real out. And perhaps the air would do him good. At least it would clear his head before he saw Aaron.

Before he had to analyze too closely *why* he was so excited to see the man.

He squeezed Jack's shoulder and got up, slipping from the room. He heard Jack murmuring something to Letty and Mrs. Merrick, his name drifting into the foyer as he walked down the hall and out the back of the house.

He sucked in air and thrust back his shoulders. Yes, he had to clear his head. And a walk was just the answer.

The two houses sat side by side, almost as connected as the men who lived inside of them were. Brothers, Jack Blackwood and Warrick, who still went by War even years after his life had been nothing but peace. Aaron Condit slowed his horse as the twin manors came into view, and he sighed.

He both dreaded and looked forward to the time he spent with Letty, who was one of his oldest friends. *Somehow* they were friends, even after all he'd done to her.

And that was the source of the dread, after all. Knowing he had hurt her so badly in the past. Her kindness was a balm and a burn at once.

Swiftly he turned his horse away from the houses and down the hill toward the lake he knew was there. He needed a few minutes more before he had to smile at Letty and shake hands with Jack and see in their eyes that they knew the truth of him.

So few people did that their knowing made him uncomfortable.

He reached the lakeside in less than five minutes and slung himself off his horse. The animal wandered off to munch on the long grass around the water's edge, and Aaron shut his eyes and took a deep breath of the warm summer air.

But if he hoped to be calmed by the action, he was sorely disappointed. For before he could sink into the breath, before he could settle into it and find some kind of peace, there was a sound behind him. A voice. A voice that made his eyes come open.

"Mr. Condit?"

He didn't have to look to know the owner of that voice. He'd known Letty's brother Griffin would be here for the party. Griffin was yet another part of the reason for Aaron's hesitation at approaching the house. But now *he* was here.

Slowly he faced the man, but no matter how he braced himself, he couldn't hold back the shudder that worked through him when he looked at Griffin. He was beautiful. With thick, dark hair that was just a touch too long, and his perfectly tailored and always dark and somber coats and waists and shiny shoes, he was a bit like a fallen angel.

Aaron knew *Griffin's* secret. He knew they shared an attraction to men. At first Aaron had been shocked when he saw him at one of the clubs that catered to such inclinations. After all, Griffin was Letty's brother, and though in the past Aaron had certainly noticed the way Griffin filled out his clothes, he'd always dismissed those thoughts.

Once he'd seen him at the Wild Boar Club in London, those thoughts had taken wing. He'd found himself staring at Griffin's mouth and wondering what it would be like to kiss it. At Griffin's broad shoulders, at his firm backside.

But the fantasies could come to nothing. Letty obviously didn't know her brother's leanings. If she did, it would likely break her heart after all she'd endured. Aaron had been a part of that once, he refused to do it a second time.

He stepped forward with a formal nod of his head. "Mr. Merrick. Letty said you would be here."

Griffin was smiling. It was such a fetching smile. A little crooked, and it revealed dimples in his cheeks. Aaron found himself wanting to step toward him, to trace that smile with his fingertip, then with his own lips.

Instead, he cleared his throat. "I hope your travels were uneventful."

Griffin's mouth continued to smile, but some of the light went out of his eyes. "My travels. Are we to talk about the roads and the weather, then?"

"Is there something else we should be discussing, Mr. Merrick?" Aaron asked, his tone slightly sharper than it should have been.

Griffin shrugged. "I suppose not. There never seems to be. My travels were fine, Mr. Condit. My mother and I came in the carriage from London and found the roads quite dry. You rode your horse and I assume found the same."

Aaron pursed his lips. He was the one who had broached the subject, but now he was annoyed by the response. "How are things coming along with your father's estate?"

That topic was far more intimate and he was rewarded by a softening of Griffin's expression. Sadness entered his eyes, trepidation.

"It has been nearly a year and it is still difficult to accept that he is gone. His estates and holdings are somewhat complicated."

Aaron did step forward now, telling himself it was only to hear better. A lie. When he did, he caught a brief whiff of Griffin's skin. He smelled of pine and clean man. There was a wild moment when he wanted to bury his nose in the crook of his neck and pull Griffin flush against him.

"H-how so?" he asked instead, trying desperately to retain his focus on matters at hand.

Griffin watched him a moment, pupils dilated as if he had read Aaron's wicked thoughts. "Father's holdings and investments are spread across nine counties, and it seems he didn't trust any one person, for there are six different managers."

Aaron pushed aside his desire with more ease. "Is there a reason for that?"

"Apparently at some point about twenty years ago, someone swindled him and he reacted by never again letting one person touch it all." Griffin sighed. "But I don't think this system of his works better."

"I could assist you," Aaron offered. The moment the words left his mouth, he wished he could take them back. Yes, he *could* help. He was a solicitor and had managed thorny estate business dozens of times in the fifteen years he had held that profession.

But offering Griffin help meant they would see each other more often. See each other in more than just passing in a club or in odd circumstances like this party. It was a bad idea.

Yet Griffin smiled again. Relief washed over his face. "Would you?" he asked. "That would be splendid. I actually have some information here, and I could send for more if you don't mind taking some time during the party."

Aaron swallowed hard. His mind was conjuring images of the two of them standing over a desk. His hand resting on Griffin's back. Sliding lower.

"Mr. Condit?" Griffin said, tilting his head.

"Yes," Aaron burst out. "That—that would be fine." He moved toward his horse before Griffin could say more. "We—*I* should go back up to the house so I can say my hellos."

Griffin nodded. "I'll go with you if you don't mind walking."

Aaron moved to gather his horse's reins. He carefully maneuvered the animal so that he was between him and Griffin. But over the animal's back, he saw Griffin's smile thin, his gaze turn away.

Aaron let out a long sigh as they walked in silence back to the house. He had apparently hurt Griffin's feelings by placing the horse between them, but what else was there to do? Between Society and their shared relationship with Letty, there would *always* be something between them.

And it was better to remember that now rather than fall into flights of fancy that there could ever be anything more than wicked, fleeting fantasies.

~

Letty laughed at something Aaron had just said, pouring him more tea and placing three lumps of sugar in it, just as he liked.

"I don't know how you stand it so sweet," she said as she passed the cup back to him. "Even after all these years."

He took a long sip. "I like it."

They were alone in the parlor. Jack had taken Griffin and gone up to the main house to join the rest of the Woodley clan. That left time for Aaron and Letty to reconnect, and he was pleased about it.

She reached across and touched his hand with a smile. "I'm so happy you came. I miss seeing you."

"As I do you. You hardly ever come to London anymore."

She shrugged. "There was never much for me there to start with, wallflower that I was. I love living out in the country. Even if I didn't, Jack is so busy with the horse breeding and breaking. He and War and Claire and I hardly have a moment to come to Town."

"Well, it leaves me at sixes and sevens," Aaron admitted. "There are friends to be had, of course, but none so good as you."

Tears brightened her eyes at the compliment he meant whole-heartedly. "We've been through quite a lot together, haven't we?"

He nodded slowly. "A lifetime's worth of things."

"Do you still think of Noah?"

Aaron stiffened at the name of his best friend, her former husband…his lover. When she had found out the truth, it had devastated her, and yet she had come to understand, perhaps in a way no one else ever had.

In the end, Noah and his death had brought Aaron and Letty together, their friendship born out of their shared love for him, as well as their shared secret of who and what Noah had been.

"Yes," he said softly. "Do you?"

To his surprise, she nodded. "Of course. He was my first husband. He was my great friend. And though we didn't suit and that brought me pain, it does not change that he meant a great deal to me during the time we were together."

Aaron sighed. In truth, Letty was the only person he could speak to about Noah. The only one who understood. It was part of why they were friends, he supposed.

"The sharpness of it has faded, but the pain remains for me."

She cleared her throat and once again her hand covered his. This time she squeezed gently, and it made him lift his gaze to hers.

"I have been wanting to speak to you for some time about a subject we tend not to broach." She leaned forward. "I worry about you, Aaron."

He let his eyes come shut gently and sat that way for a moment, trying to find peace. Comfort. "Worry? Why?" he said, allowing himself to look at her once more.

"You lock yourself away, busying yourself with work. Do you keep *any* company?"

His eyes widened. "Are you asking if I have a…a lover?"

Her cheeks colored dark red and she turned her face slightly. "I don't know that I would have been that blunt, though I suppose that *is* what I meant. A lover, yes, for that physical connection is important. But I think I meant more of a companion. A friend. Someone you care for and who cares for you in return?"

Aaron's mind slipped, against his will, to thoughts of Griffin. Griffin's smile, which seemed to draw his own out of the cobwebs and shadows. But *that* was not possible.

He drew in a long breath. "No, Letty. No one like that."

Her frown drew down deeply. "You must be very lonely."

He had nothing to say, so he remained silent, focusing on a stray thread at the wrist of his jacket rather than her stare. That didn't mean he wasn't aware of it, though. Nor of her true and very sweet concern.

When he didn't reply, she sighed. "Oh Aaron, Noah would not want this for you. I know he wouldn't."

"I suppose he would not," Aaron agreed softly. "But it's not as easy for men like me."

"I realize that," she whispered.

He lifted his gaze to her, and this time he knew his smile had a touch of condescension. He couldn't help it when she spoke of things she couldn't possibly know.

"You *think* you do," he said. "What I do, what I am…it isn't something I can change. It has hurt, it has destroyed. You were a casualty of it. I could be, as well, thanks to the laws of our land. So even if I could meet someone, why would I *ever* risk doing that again?"

"Couldn't it be different this time?"

Once again, Aaron's thoughts shifted to Griffin. He doubted Letty knew about her younger brother's predilections. If she did… well, even as accepting as she was, he knew it would hurt her. As would Aaron's giving in to his desires. It would be another betrayal of Letty. His best friend.

And he wouldn't do that.

"No," he said, rising. "It wouldn't. Now please, don't worry yourself about this. Why don't we join the others at the main house? I promise I will not bring the party down with my brooding."

"That wasn't my concern," Letty said, rising. "And you know it."

He leaned in to buss her cheek and smiled. "Of course it wasn't, my dearest Letty. Now come on, I could use a walk to clear my head."

She smiled as she took the arm he offered, but he felt her tension as they left the parlor and headed for the front door. Worse, he felt his own. Coming here when he knew Griffin would be in attendance had been a mistake.

And all he could do was try to avoid making even more of them.

CHAPTER 2

Griffin shifted in discomfort as he looked around the ballroom. It was packed with guests, both family and others. Normally these types of gatherings were boring and stuffy, but with all the Woodleys, Flynns and Blackwoods in attendance, there was a much more relaxed environment. Pairs of them spun by, laughing in each other's arms. All the married couples looked blissfully happy.

Griffin's neck itched at the sight of it. He felt so outside of it all.

"You are scowling," Mrs. Merrick said as she sidled up to him with her former sister-in-law—the once Lady Woodley, but now Mrs. Gray—at her side.

"Hello, Mama," Griffin said, bending to kiss first her cheek, then turning to his aunt. "Aunt Susanna."

"You are handsome as ever, darling," his aunt said, squeezing of his hand. "Serious scowl or not."

"I'm sorry if I appear out of sorts," he said, trying to force something resembling a smile on his face.

It was almost impossible to do. Everyone else in the room was practically radiating their deep and abiding love for their spouses, and he could see the sparkle in his mother's eyes that said she was about to push him toward dancing. God, how he hated dancing.

Thanks to the overcrowded room and the circumstances, he was hot and uncomfortable and ill-tempered in every way.

And, of course, none of those things were the real reason for his discomfort. Aaron Condit had been avoiding him for twenty-four hours. He exited rooms when Griffin entered. He stepped away if he saw Griffin coming. He didn't sit beside him at supper, nor did he come near him if they were in a room with the others.

Griffin had no idea why. No one in the household knew of their shared…*issues*, so they would never be suspected of anything if they spent time together. But perhaps Aaron didn't like him. Griffin had often thought he did. Sometimes he caught Aaron watching him in clubs, and he'd thought when they spoke down by the lake the previous day that there had been some kind of spark between them.

But it seemed that wasn't true, and he was beginning to feel frustrated and foolish about it.

"Look, there is Lady—" his mother began.

Griffin leaned in to grab her hand, and squeezed gently. "You know, Mama, my head is spinning in this crush. Why don't you let me take a turn on the terrace to clear it, and then I promise I will come inside and dance twice tonight."

His mother's eyes narrowed. "Three times."

He sighed as he turned away to make his escape. "Of course, three times."

"With different partners, and your cousins and your sister don't count," she called after him.

He lifted a hand to indicate he understood and that he surrendered, and hurried away before she added even more conditions to the rest of his evening.

He pushed the terrace doors open and stepped into the cool night air with a sigh. He shut the doors behind him and walked to the edge of the precipice where he fisted his hands against the edge of the stone wall and leaned there, his head bent.

"I wouldn't recommend jumping."

He lifted his head at the voice that came from behind him. Aaron. Slowly, he turned.

"I wouldn't do something so foolish," he said, keeping his tone as neutral as he could when Aaron came out of the shadows, and Griffin's heart leapt.

God, but Aaron was handsome. Ridiculously handsome. He had dark blond hair and a neatly trimmed beard—Griffin had wondered over and over what it would feel like brushing over bare skin. Aaron also had dark eyes that often spoke of deep sadness. Deep loss, though Griffin had never had the nerve to talk to him about it. They never spoke of anything more intimate than the weather.

Aaron's doing.

"I thought you *loved* to dance," Griffin said, flicking his head toward the ballroom.

Aaron shook his head. "I just pretend better than you do."

"Well, we are both practiced enough at it," Griffin mumbled as he forced himself to look over the garden again. "Pretending, not dancing."

Aaron surprised him by stepping up beside him and placing his own hands on the wall. If Griffin leaned his little finger out, he could brush it over Aaron's.

"Still, I have a good many years on you. You must be a decade younger than I am," Aaron said.

That was true. Griffin knew Aaron was older than Letty, but who gave a damn about that? If Griffin were a woman no one would blink at the ten years separating them.

Griffin shrugged. "I suppose I never thought of our age difference. It isn't age that makes it complicated between us, is it?"

Beside him, Aaron sucked in a great breath before he pivoted to face Griffin. Griffin did the same, his heart suddenly pounding. They were standing very close. So close that it would hardly take a thing to touch him.

"Griffin," Aaron said softly, his voice rough.

Griffin jolted. Aaron always referred to him as Mr. Merrick.

Now his given name rolled off the other man's tongue, as intimate as a caress. But Aaron was going to reject him. Griffin could see it. He wasn't ready for it.

"What say we take a brief turn about the garden?" he suggested, taking a step back. "To help me avoid my fate."

Aaron opened and shut his mouth, as if trying to formulate a response, then sighed. "What fate is that?"

"My mother has negotiated that I dance three times tonight, none of them with my married friends or family. So the longer you help me stay out here, the more you save me."

Aaron's pupils dilated in the moonlight. "You want me to save you?"

Griffin swallowed hard. "I would owe you a favor."

A slow smile spread over Aaron's face, and then he nodded. "I-I suppose there would be no harm in a walk. Lead the way."

Griffin stepped out and moved toward the set of stone steps on the opposite side of the terrace. Aaron walked at his side, quiet in the still night air. Griffin watched him with a few furtive glances. Aaron was very graceful. There was a strength and a power to him, yes, but it was a lithe and lean strength. Like he could dance his movements and no one would dare question it.

They maneuvered their way through the dark pathways of the garden, illuminated only be a few lamps. The sounds of the party slowly faded away in the distance and finally silenced entirely as they reached a gazebo far off from the house. During the daytime, it offered a perfect overlook to the lake. At night Griffin could imagine its cushioned seats had provided many a private escape for a pair of lovers.

He shuddered as they entered the little building. Aaron edged away from him, taking a seat and refusing to look at him.

"Why don't we ever speak about seeing each other in London?" Griffin asked.

He hadn't intended to say those words and he fought a desperate urge to clap a hand over his mouth and wish them back.

Slowly Aaron lifted his gaze to his. "Because no good will come of it," he whispered.

Griffin wrinkled a brow. "How is that possible? You and I already know each other. That we share such urges is a binding factor, whether we speak a syllable about it or not. At least if we could discuss it I wouldn't feel so..."

He trailed away, cutting off his vulnerability before he could reveal the entirety of his soft underbelly. In truth, he didn't fully trust Aaron not to cut him.

Aaron stared at him for a long, charged moment, then stood. "Feel so what?"

Griffin swallowed, struggling with his words. Then he whispered, "Alone."

Aaron's jaw tightened, like he was gritting his teeth. He took another long step toward Griffin, his eyes flashing emotion. Griffin at first thought it was anger, and he recoiled. But the closer Aaron came, the more he realized that wasn't it at all.

"Have you ever thought that the reason I don't discuss this with you is because I fear I would not just talk to you?" Aaron said softly. "Have you ever considered that perhaps it is self-preservation?"

"What do you mean you wouldn't just talk to me?" Griffin asked, even though his heart was pounding with excitement. He knew exactly what Aaron meant. He meant he was afraid that if they spoke of things plainly that he would...*touch* Griffin.

"Fuck," Aaron said, and turned to leave the gazebo.

Griffin caught his arm before he could go and spun him back. Aaron tensed, as if ready to pull away, perhaps even ready to fight, but before he could do any of it Griffin leaned in and pressed his lips to Aaron's.

For a moment, the world stopped. Both men froze, their mouths locked. Griffin could feel the tension in Aaron's body, the fight he was waging. Then he mumbled a curse against Griffin's mouth and grabbed his arms, dragging him closer as he opened and slanted his mouth to deepen the kiss.

Griffin opened too, and their tongues met, tangling with desperate passion, with long withheld curiosity and desire. Griffin had often wondered what Aaron would taste like. It turned out it was mint and whiskey, and the combination made his toes curl in his shoes as he drank deeply of the heady mixture.

Aaron clung to Griffin's arms, his fingers biting into his biceps as his tongue plunged hard and fast, mimicking a fuck and making Griffin tremble with anticipation. He managed to rip his arms free of Aaron's grip and wrapped them around him, their bodies molding from head to toe.

He felt Aaron's fingers gliding along his spine and he shuddered at the pleasure that touch caused, even through all the heavy layers of wool and cotton that separated them. His cock swelled and he arched, driving his tongue harder into Aaron's mouth. His erection bumped Aaron's and they both shuddered at the slide of cock on cock.

They rocked like that, rubbing lightly as the kiss slowed, gentled. There was no longer a war between them, just a desire to touch, to be close, to sate the need that had been born that first moment their eyes met across the room at a forbidden club. Griffin felt like he was melting, melting, merging with Aaron, two now an inseparable one. He slid his hands down Aaron's back and cupped his backside, drawing him up tighter to increase the pleasure of rubbing cocks.

Aaron froze at the action, his lips ceasing their movement, his hips tensing.

"No," he mumbled against Griffin's mouth.

Griffin drew back slightly. "Please," he whispered.

"No," Aaron repeated, this time more strenuously. He pulled from Griffin's arms and paced across the gazebo. His shoulders shook as he ran a hand through his thick blond hair, and he refused to turn back to look at Griffin.

"Why?" Griffin asked, his voice shaking as hard as his body. "Why not? We both know this is what we are, what we do. And we both know there has been an attraction between us—not just in the past day, but for far longer than that."

Aaron spun at that. His mouth was drawn down in a deep frown. "Yes," he admitted. "Yes, all of that is true. But I can't. Not with you."

"Damn it," Griffin snapped out, gripping his hands at his sides. "What the hell is wrong with me that I don't rise to your standards of who to fuck?"

Aaron's lips parted in surprise at the strong words. He rocked like he was going to move toward Griffin, but he dripped his head and instead stepped back. "I-I can't because…because I won't hurt your sister. Not like that. Not again."

~

Aaron watched as Griffin's mouth dropped open in surprise at his outburst. He couldn't blame him. Aaron was a bit surprised by it, too. He had never spoken to anyone about his past with Letty and Noah. But the kiss…that glorious kiss had changed everything.

The moment Griffin touched him, Aaron's mind had emptied of everything but pleasure. Of need for this man that he had tried to stifle, to ignore, to destroy. It was impossible, though. He wanted Griffin so fucking much that it hurt. A deep, soul hurt that he recognized.

He had felt it once before. And it had ended so badly.

"Don't just stare at me," Griffin demanded through clenched teeth. "Explain what you mean."

Aaron squeezed his eyes shut. As much as he wanted to avoid it, he had to tell the truth. It was the only way to make Griffin understand *why* they couldn't be together. The only way to stop this out of control boulder racing down the hill toward them. He opened his eyes and met Griffin's.

"Do you know my history?" he asked, his voice choked and croaking.

Griffin cocked his head. "A little. You are a solicitor. You're the best friend of Letty's late first husband, Lord Seagate. You want the same things I do, even if you stand here saying you don't want *me*."

The last sentence was said harshly, an accusation that stung Aaron to his core.

He rubbed a hand over his face. "Noah and I met as children, and yes, we were friends. But by the time I was sixteen, I knew that I was…*different*. That I couldn't deny these urges that swelled inside of me. I felt like I was drowning and I resolved to kill myself."

He saw Griffin's throat work as he swallowed hard. Saw a darkness enter his eyes that Aaron knew so well. Perhaps Griffin understood his past a bit more than Aaron had guessed. Perhaps Griffin, too, had felt the pain when what he wanted seemed so huge and lonely and impossible.

"But you didn't," Griffin said softly.

"No, I didn't. Noah caught me about to follow through, and he stopped me."

Aaron pictured Noah, just a year older than he had been, storming into his room and snatching the gun from his hands. Pictured Noah grabbing him and dragging him to his feet to hold him. How they had both shook with terror at what they had nearly lost.

"You told him what you were?" Griffin encouraged.

"Not exactly." Aaron shivered. "He kissed me. And I realized that I *wasn't* alone."

Griffin caught his breath, his face twisting in shock and then horror as those words sank in. "Wait, you and Noah…you and my sister's husband…"

"Were lovers for many years," Aaron admitted. "And not just lovers. I *loved* him to my core, and I know he loved me. But he was titled and there were expectations. Hence Letty. The moment he proposed, we vowed to stay away from each other. To only be friends. But we couldn't. We *couldn't*. He hated himself for coming to me. I hated myself for letting him in. But we did it anyway."

"Does Letty know?" Griffin asked. "Does she have any idea?"

Aaron smiled sadly. "Oh yes. She saw us, you see. And it all came out in a horrible rush. How I despised her at the time for being able to freely have what I could not. And she hated me for taking what he couldn't give her. It was an untenable situation, made worse by… well, there were a great many things that made it worse that I won't get into because Letty is your sister."

Griffin flinched at the intimate implications of those words. "But you are friends now. I don't recall a time when you weren't. How did that happen?"

"You know Letty," Aaron whispered. "Can't you guess? She watched Noah suffer with his true self and she saw how much our being parted hurt us both. And then Noah got so very sick and…" He caught his breath as pain mobbed him. "In the end, we were bound be our twin grief. She for the husband she never truly had. Me for the man I could never freely love."

Griffin was silent for a beat and then he sighed. "Of course…of course she would do that. Letty is…"

"Amazing," Aaron finished with a soft smile for the friend he loved so completely. "When she fell in love with Jack, when it became clear that there would be the happiest of endings for her, there was no one who celebrated as much as I did."

Griffin's brow knitted. "You hurt Letty by your actions with Noah, but why does that interfere with us?"

Aaron stared at him. "How can you ask me that? Does Letty know what you are? Who you fuck? Where you go in London?"

Griffin's face went tight and it answered the question even before he ground out, "No."

"So you would have me hurt her all over again? I took her husband and now I would take her beloved younger brother?" Aaron sighed. "You are younger than I am—perhaps you haven't seen or done as much. Let me tell you, it is better to hide what we are."

Griffin lifted his chin. "I've been hiding what I am for years.

Don't say I haven't suffered for it. Or that it doesn't cause just as much pain. It sent me looking for any kind of acceptance, it sent me seeking out the kind of life Jack Blackwood used to live. My mistakes in trying to find my place nearly got my sister and her husband killed."

Aaron arched a brow. He knew the story, of course—he had been part of it. "Then you have hurt her and I have hurt her. Doing it all again would be far too much. I won't do it, Griffin. I...I won't."

Aaron moved toward the exit, but before he left, he turned back. Griffin was standing in the same spot where they'd kissed, his face pale, his hands gripped at his sides. Everything in Aaron screamed at him to go back. Not to walk away from the intensity of feeling he hadn't experienced since the horrible moment when Noah breathed his last.

"I'm sorry," Aaron said, choking on the words.

Griffin said nothing, just stared at him, and Aaron could take it no longer. He fled the gazebo, fled the lighted path beside it, fled into the dark garden so he wouldn't have to face everything he wanted.

And everything he stood to lose by saying no.

CHAPTER 3

Griffin paused at the breakfast room door and allowed himself a long, deep sigh. Inside, there were gales of laughter, voices all chattering at once. He stood outside, wishing he could just slink away and never come back.

But he couldn't, so he opened the door and came inside, placing a false smile on his face. The moment he entered the room, that smile was tested. Aaron sat at the table, wedged between two misses whose names Griffin couldn't recall, despite having been introduced to them last night and even dancing with one of them.

Aaron glanced up when he entered, his gaze sliding to Griffin slowly. His face pinched in what appeared to be pain, regret, and then he looked away. Griffin pressed his lips together tighter as annoyance gripped him.

Aaron was going to pretend none of it had ever happened. Aaron was going to deny the attraction between them. And now Griffin knew the reasons, but they still stung.

"Good morning, Griffin," Letty said, moving away from the sideboard to press a kiss on his cheek.

Griffin swallowed hard. *There* was the reason for Aaron's withdrawal. Letty, who loved them both so desperately. Letty, who had suffered at both their hands because of their secrets. Just as he had when he returned to the ball last night, he found himself examining her face more closely, trying to find the scars those actions had left behind. She hid them well.

And he should know, being an expert at hiding.

Her expression wavered slightly when he didn't respond to her greeting for far too long. "Are you well?"

He shook off his thoughts and reached out to squeeze her hand gently. "Of course. Just realizing I don't often stay up so late, nor dance nearly so much as I did last night."

She patted his arm, accepting his excuse, then returned to the table to take her place next to Jack. Griffin filled his plate, despite the fact that he wasn't hungry in the slightest, and took the last remaining place at the table between his mother and the father of one of the eligible young ladies she was attempting to feed him to.

"Good morning, darling," Mrs. Merrick said.

"Good morning, Mama," he said, working hard to keep his mind on matters at hand and not stare like a moonfaced fool at Aaron down the table. "I trust you slept well."

"I did," she said with a bright smile. "When I left last night, you were still dancing, which pleased me greatly."

Griffin ducked his head. Oh yes, he had danced. When he returned to the party, so tight with anger and disappointment, he had thrown himself into the duty of dancing with three different women, as his mother desired. And three had turned to five, then ten. He had likely danced with every young woman in attendance.

As if it were penance.

Only his soul didn't feel particularly cleansed. His feet just hurt.

"Well, I know my reluctance is a difficulty for you," he said, forcing himself to take a bite of his food and chew its sawdust consistency slowly.

"Not a difficulty," she corrected, looking at him with kindness, gentleness, love. "I only wish for you to be happy. I know you're a young man yet, with time to settle down. But with your father gone,

I realize it is hard for you. A partner in your life might make it easier."

Griffin stared at her in wonder. His parents were not like the Woodleys, despite his father and the late Lord Woodley being brothers. They weren't warm and welcoming and overflowing with love. They'd been more traditional parents, more distant and proper, both with each other and with their children.

So to hear Mrs. Merrick speak to him of her hopes for his future was a surprise.

"I would very much like that kind of partner, Mama," he said, and he meant it. How he would love to find the kind of bond that Letty had with Jack. But for him that felt...impossible. Especially considering last night. "But it isn't so very easy, is it?"

There was a flutter to his mother's face and she bent her head. "No, I suppose it isn't. But we'll keep looking, won't we? Keep trying."

He forced the same smile that had been so difficult a moment ago. It was no less so now as he lied, "Of course. I'll keep looking."

She seemed appeased by that and turned her attention to the lady on her opposite side. They began to chat and Griffin went back to his food. But her words sank in. They had meaning, even if it wasn't the kind she hoped for.

There was only one person with whom who he knew he could share the kind of partnership she described. Aaron had already offered to help Griffin as he shuffled through the difficult and complicated mess his father had left behind in his estates. Griffin could easily picture them unknotting the thorny tendrils of his duty together and afterward sharing a drink and a laugh and a kiss like the one last night.

They would be well matched, and he knew it. He allowed himself to glance down the table at Aaron and found him staring back. Griffin held the gaze evenly, almost daring Aaron to look away.

At last he did, and Griffin shook his head. He wanted Aaron so much—not just his body, but something more. And yet it was clear that would be impossible because of the past, because of the present, because of a future that wouldn't allow them to entangle their lives.

It was so bloody unfair.

Letty rose from her place at the end of the table as the servants cleared away the rest of the dishes, and smiled at the group. "This morning Claire and I have devised a little fun for everyone."

Jack laughed. "Tell War that."

She waved her hand at him. "Stop. We have put together a scavenger hunt. Around the estate, we have hidden two treasures. One for the men, one for the women. Once we all take the walk up to the main house, we shall pair off and go on the hunt. First pair to win shares the prize."

The room was filled with chattering and laughter as everyone rose and servants began to come with gloves and hats and shawls.

Griffin sighed at the cacophony of sound. No doubt he would be paired with some eligible miss, his mother's and sister's not-so-subtle attempt to wed him off. He would spend the afternoon smiling and holding her hand and feel absolutely nothing. It seemed an unfair exercise for them both.

But he got to his feet and accepted his gloves, which he shoved in his pocket rather than put on. He felt constricted enough right now, he didn't need more layers of fabric to add to the sensation.

He trailed after the group as they piled onto the drive and began to short walk up the hill toward the Woodley manor. It was his cousin Edward's home, of course, but his aunt Susanna and her current husband, Mr. Jed Gray, lived in it now. Yet another blissfully happy couple.

"I have a question, Mrs. Blackwood," came a female voice from Griffin's left.

He turned his head to find a pretty brunette was the one who had spoken. She sent him a half smile before Letty said, "What is it, Miss Porter?"

"You mentioned there would be a prize for the men and one for the women. Does that mean the winning pair must find both?"

Letty tossed her another quick smile before she said, "Oh no, you misunderstand. The pairs will not be a man and a woman. This is a battle of the sexes. Women *versus* the men."

Griffin jerked his gaze to Aaron, who had folded himself into the crowd ahead. Aaron's shoulders stiffened, but he kept walking without looking back.

"Oh," Miss Porter said, her lower lip extending slightly in a pout. "I see."

The crowd murmured as one while they made the rest of the walk to the house, disappointment and excitement seeming to rise in equal measure depending on the relationships involved or the grasping of the mamas for a match.

On the other hand, Griffin felt two things at this development. One was relief. He wouldn't be forced to squire around a young lady who was interested in his purse and his name. The other was a thrill of excitement. Although the party was a large one, there was still a possibility that he might be paired with Aaron.

And if that happened, Aaron wouldn't be able to avoid continuing their conversation from last night. Because it needed continuing, and Griffin was not about to be put off.

Aaron watched as Letty stood on the steps of the veranda, looking down over the crowd gathered in the garden. It was a lively group of laughing, happy people, excited to get the day's events started.

He, on the other hand, felt sick as he watched Jack hand over a top hat which had been filled with scraps of paper with each man's name on them. The women had already been paired from an equally designed bonnet and gathered back, giggling as they plotted their plans of attack.

He wanted to be paired with anyone, anyone at all, just not Griffin. Aaron could feel him standing behind him. Feel his stare boring into his back. And Aaron's body liked it, damn it. His body wanted what his mind could not.

"Warrick will be with…" Letty laughed as she dug into the hat to retrieve a second name. "Mr. Gray."

Aaron huffed out a breath as Letty's huge brother-in-law moved over to her aunt's husband and the two shook hands. War didn't look particularly happy to play games, but he still shot Claire a heated looked. She nodded and called out, "May the best Blackwood win!"

"Thank you!" he called back, inspiring a quick bubble of laughter through the crowd.

Aaron's stomach clenched at their easy connection. They were so lucky in it and didn't even know.

"Ah, and here is Griffin's name," Letty said, lifting the paper from the hat with a smile. "Who shall be paired with…"

The pause as she dug into the hat seemed to stretch for a lifetime. Finally she pulled a folded sheet from the hat. Aaron squeezed his eyes shut.

Please. Please. Please.

"Aaron Condit," she said, and he opened his eyes to watch her lips forming the syllables of his name in slow motion.

His heart began to throb as he looked over his shoulder at Griffin. He was coming toward Aaron in what felt like equally slow motion, his dark eyes focused on Aaron's face, his full lips turned up in what almost looked like a smirk.

After last night Griffin couldn't possibly be happy with this pairing. And yet as he reached him, Griffin held out a hand. "I look forward to what we'll find together," he said, his deep voice seductive.

Aaron sucked in a breath and slowly reached for the hand extended toward him. Griffin wasn't wearing gloves, nor was he, so when their palms touched to shake hands it was skin on skin and a jolt of electric desire worked through him.

Letty had moved on to the next pairing and Griffin shifted to stand beside him, calm and seemingly unmoved by what had just happened. Meanwhile, Aaron felt like he would come out of his skin.

"And that's the last," Letty said after calling the last two names. "Claire and I will dole out the first clue for your hunts. We will meet back here in two hours, so if you cannot find anything or you don't hear this call—" She motioned to a servant, who rang a huge gong that had been placed on the terrace above them. "—then return here at that time. Good luck."

As Letty grabbed for a pile of envelopes and Claire took another, they began to circulate through the crowd. There were some who tore into their clues with gusto and immediately took off across the grounds. When Letty handed Aaron their envelope, she smiled. "Good luck."

Aaron sighed and turned toward Griffin, holding out the envelope with embarrassingly shaky hands. "Do you want to do the honor?"

Griffin reached out and took the envelope, but his fingers slid across Aaron's in what could only be a purposeful attempt at intimacy. Aaron didn't want to, but his body reacted to that grazing touch, clenching and hardening. He glared at Griffin, who smiled back as if he were innocent.

"Certainly," he said, breaking the seal on the envelope and pulling out a neatly printed sheet. "Shall I read it out loud?"

Aaron nodded, not trusting his voice to do anything else.

"'Just a building, not a home. You might go there to be alone. You might go there to find a friend. You might go where the creek ends.'"

Aaron blinked. "I've no idea."

Griffin folded the paper and slid it into his waistcoat pocket. "I know. Come on."

Aaron fell into step behind him as the Griffin led him to the same path where everyone else was racing. But after they'd walked with the others for a while, Griffin turned and stepped off the path and into the woods.

Aaron wrinkled his brow and followed slowly. "This isn't where anyone else is going."

Griffin gave him a look over his shoulder. "Well, then no one else has figured out the clue. *I* know exactly where to go."

Aaron took a few long steps and fell in beside Griffin. They walked in silence for a while, but Aaron wouldn't have called it companionable. There was tension between them, pulsing and heated, both frustrated and filled with desire.

Why the hell did they have to have been matched?

They'd walked for a good ten minutes, stepping over fallen logs and through brambles before Aaron stopped and folded his arms.

"All right, where are you taking me?"

Griffin laughed before he reached back and caught Aaron's hand. Their fingers threaded naturally, and Griffin tugged.

"Just a little farther, I promise."

Aaron could hardly breathe as he looked down at their intimately entwined fingers. Griffin's hand was warm, and every once in a while he would smooth his thumb over Aaron's palm, sending shockwaves of awareness through him.

"Here," Griffin said.

Aaron blinked. He'd almost forgotten their purpose in being here, but now he looked down a short hill to where the creek bubbled toward…

"The icehouse," he breathed.

Griffin grinned. "Indeed it is. Come on."

They climbed down the small hill together and stopped just in front of the small stone building.

"How did you guess this?" Aaron asked as Griffin released his hand and began searching around them for their next clue in the game.

Griffin glanced up at Aaron, his dark gaze grabbing Aaron's for a brief moment. "Oh, it wasn't hard. The icehouse is where I often went to be alone when my family visited the Woodleys. And it was a meeting place for *all* the boys when we wanted to get up to mischief."

Aaron blinked. "That seems like a rather specific clue to the family. How will the gentlemen who aren't part of the Woodley clan discover it? And why aren't all your male cousins swarming on the place?"

Griffin had been bent over a loose rock at the back of the little house, but now he straightened and looked around. The woods were still, they couldn't even hear the calls of the other players anymore. His brow wrinkled.

"I don't know. Perhaps each pairing got different clues."

Aaron shook his head. "That would seem a bit unfair."

"Well, it's a game, Aaron," Griffin said with a long sigh as he went back to searching. "You take everything so damned seriously."

Aaron stiffened at the accusatory tone that had nothing to do with their search. He took a few long steps toward Griffin, his hands flexed at his sides.

"Don't judge me, Griffin."

Griffin stood again and glared at him. "Why shouldn't I? After all, you're making decisions for both of us now. I suppose I get to be angry or disappointed or frustrated by them."

"I'm *not* making decisions for you."

"Aren't you?" Griffin asked, and he reached out to catch Aaron's hand, tugging him forward. The ground was uneven, so Aaron stumbled and suddenly he was in Griffin's arms. He looked up into Griffin's face, taut with desire, and his stomach flipped.

"Isn't this making decisions for *me*?" he whispered.

Griffin didn't answer, but bent his head and pressed his lips to Aaron's. Aaron should have recoiled, or pushed against Griffin's chest, or said no. But he didn't. Instead, he opened his mouth and allowed Griffin in, just as he had the night before.

Their tongues tangled and Griffin fisted Aaron's coat, dragging him even closer, until their bodies were flush against each other and Aaron could feel the pulsing need in Griffin's hard cock. It mimicked his own, which was at full mast now and aching to take what he had sworn he would never give.

Griffin backed him up, guiding him until Aaron's backside hit the cool smoothness of the icehouse wall. His eyes flew open then and he found Griffin's face mere inches from his.

Griffin didn't break the gaze, but held steady as he slid his hands down Aaron's chest, over his hips, and then unbuttoned the first fastening on his trousers.

Aaron's hips bucked against his will, but he shook his head. "If the others come…"

"We're at the back of the building," Griffin said softly, unhooking the next button. "We'll hear them before they see us if they do come."

Aaron squeezed his eyes shut as Griffin made swift work of the final buttons at the fly and then slipped a hand into Aaron's trousers. His fingers folded around Aaron's cock and he tugged, freeing it gently.

"Oh God," Aaron moaned, unable to do anything else as Griffin stroked his hand over him once, twice, three times.

"Tell me you want me," Griffin ordered.

Aaron opened his eyes to find Griffin staring at him, his expression wild and primal and filled with heat and desire. Slowly he nodded. "God help me, I do want you, Griffin Merrick."

"Good," Griffin breathed before he dropped down to his knees.

Aaron's gaze went wide as he watched Griffin stroke his thumb back and forth over the swollen head of Aaron's cock. It felt fantastic, but he wanted something more. He wanted Griffin's mouth. As if he read that desire, Griffin looked up at him as he lowered his lips to Aaron's erection.

Wet heat swirled around Aaron, and he let out a groan that seemed to echo in the air. He reached down to slide his fingers into the crisp shortness of Griffin's hair and rested his head back against the icehouse wall with a thump as Griffin began to suck.

Griffin's tongue swirled around his length in slow, firm circles, even as he squeezed the base of Aaron's cock gently. All of Aaron's focus, all of his attempts to hold back, faded and his entire world became centered on this man's mouth. His magical mouth that now began to pump over Aaron slowly, drawing him farther in with each stroke.

Aaron found his hips flexing, taking Griffin's mouth gently in the utter quiet of the woods. It felt amazing, it felt perfect, it felt right as Griffin pumped harder, faster, pulling pleasure from every fiber of Aaron's being until his entire body felt like it was tingling, perching on the edge.

He was going to come. Right here in the middle of the forest, with Griffin Merrick's mouth latched around him. He grunted, trying to pull away, but Griffin wouldn't allow it. If anything, he sucked harder, and Aaron's vision blurred as he let out a long, harsh moan of pleasure and pumped his seed deep into Griffin's throat.

Griffin took it all, even as he smiled up at Aaron. Only when Aaron sagged against the building, sated with release, did he pull him free from Griffin's lips. Gently, he tucked Aaron back into place and buttoned him, then got to his feet and leaned in to kiss him deeply.

Aaron tasted his release on Griffin's tongue and drew their bodies flush together, wondering what Griffin would taste like. Wanting to test it, to tease him as he'd just been teased.

Fuck, he was starting to get hard again just thinking about it.

Griffin pulled away at last and smiled at him. "I think I found our prize."

Aaron squeezed his eyes shut. Griffin's words had only served to remind him of what the consequences of their actions were. Of the stakes at hand.

"Griffin," he began, but Griffin leaned in and pressed his fingers to Aaron's lips.

"I understand your hesitation," Griffin said, wrapping his arms around Aaron's waist and leaning against him. The weight of him was a comfort when it shouldn't have been.

"Letty means a great deal to me," Aaron whispered, his voice breaking.

"And she means the world to me. But there is no denying that what is between us is powerful. Is there?"

Aaron knew he should say he could deny it. That what had happened just now was a slip and nothing more. But he couldn't form the words. They were a lie. "I can't deny it," he admitted.

Griffin nodded. "Then the best thing for us to do might be to give in. To purge this thing between us. So just…let me. For a little while, just *let* me."

Aaron bent his head. He wasn't strong enough to say no. Not now that he had felt Griffin's mouth around him. Not now when he wanted to give him just as much pleasure in return. Pandora's Box had been opened.

"Very well," he whispered, ignoring how Griffin's face lit up when he said it. "But we must be careful."

"Very careful," Griffin agreed, leaning in to kiss him once more before he backed away. "Now, what say we find out next clue?"

Aaron nodded and moved toward the front of the icehouse. "Yes. That would probably be best."

Only he knew neither of them was thinking of what was *best* right now. He only hoped giving in to passion wouldn't cause worse problems in the future.

CHAPTER 4

Griffin sat at his aunt's long supper table and couldn't help but smile. His thoughts kept drifting back to those moments with Aaron at the icehouse that afternoon. Touching him, tasting him, making him convulse with pleasure…damn, but a man could live on those moments.

"You look very pleased for a man who did not win the prize at the scavenger hunt today," Jack Blackwood said, elbowing him to motion to the small medal now pinned to his chest. A matching one for the ladies teams was pinned to his cousin Evan's wife Josie's gown.

Griffin arched a brow. "I'm fairly certain you cheated," he teased. "And is that just a farthing with a pin attached?"

Jack grinned as he reached up to touch the award. "You never know when a farthing will come in handy, Griffin. This could well be a lifesaving reward someday."

Griffin bowed his head as if to concede the point. Then he looked down the table at Letty, who was chatting with Aaron. Seeing her talk to him and now knowing what she'd been through was sobering. She was so forgiving, even in the face of pain.

"Letty looks happy," Griffin said with a smile.

Jack nodded and his face lit up with pleasure. "I hate these gatherings—give me dinner with one friend at a time over this. But she adores arranging and planning. It is her nature to take care of everyone in the room."

Griffin tensed at those words. "Yes, it seems that is true. She's always been that way, reaching out to those who needed it."

Jack let out a long breath. "Your father once told me she liked to collect birds with broken wings. He was, of course, referring to me being one of them."

Griffin glanced at his brother-in-law. "He grew to like you, though."

"Indeed, he did, and I him." Jack frowned. "You have a great deal more responsibility now that he's gone."

Griffin nodded. "Yes. And it's...*complicated*. But Aaron—Mr. Condit—has offered to assist so that takes some of the pressure off my mind. Do you...do you think Letty would approve of our friendship?"

Jack looked at Aaron and Letty, and shrugged. "Letty will approve of anything that will make you happy or more at ease. You know that."

Perhaps the answer should have made Griffin feel better, but it didn't. Jack's words were a reminder that not only did Letty do everything to make others happy, but she sometimes did it at a deficit to herself. If she found out what was truly between him and Aaron, would that hurt her? Would she even tell him if it did?

Those were Aaron's fears, of course. And they were valid. Yet even with all that on his mind, Griffin still wanted Aaron with a power that was actually terrifying. One taste hadn't been enough. He wanted more.

And they'd already promised to be careful.

Jack patted his arm as Letty sent him a nod down the table. "I suppose I have a duty to do now, excuse me." He rose to his feet. "Gentlemen, why don't we retire to the Blue Room for port? We'll join the ladies later in the Green Room."

Everyone rose and began to move, the rustle of gowns and the murmur of voices filling the space. Jack stepped forward to speak to his brother War, and the others began to walk out of the room to their various parlors when Griffin finally got up. As he did so, he caught Aaron watching him from the corner of his eye.

Griffin moved toward him with a small smile that Aaron didn't return. He fell into step beside him and said, "Did you enjoy supper?"

Aaron bobbed out a curt nod. "I did."

"The soup was especially good."

Aaron shot him a glare. "What does *that* mean?"

Griffin blinked at the defensiveness of his tone. "That I…like…pea…soup?" he said slowly.

Aaron stared straight ahead. "I see. Perhaps we shouldn't be seen talking to each other."

Griffin looked around. They were the last in the line of gentlemen going to the parlor, the ladies had already peeled off to go to their gathering place.

"No one is even paying attention to us, Aaron."

Aaron stopped and turned on Griffin. His lips were pinched. "But they could. And I don't want anyone to talk. To see."

Griffin caught his arm and dragged him toward the billiard room behind them. He pushed the door shut and leaned against it, staring at the man he had given pleasure to just a few hours before. Aaron wouldn't even meet his eyes now.

"You're afraid they're going to see that we want each other," Griffin said softly.

Aaron nodded. "Yes. Yes, because I am having a hard time hiding it."

Griffin's lips parted at that admission, and he moved toward Aaron in one long step. He reached out and caught Aaron's hand, pulling him a little closer. Until they were a breath apart.

"Come to my room tonight," he whispered.

Aaron squeezed his eyes shut, clearly caught between what he wanted and what he felt was right. "No," he said, his voice shaking.

Griffin cupped Aaron's chin, letting his thumb stroke across his full lower lip and feeling Aaron's breath hitch. "Please," he murmured. "Please."

Aaron's entire body was tense, and for a long moment he was silent. But finally he let out a long, deep sigh. "Very well. I'll come to you after midnight."

"I'll leave my door unlocked," Griffin promised.

Aaron stepped back, breaking the contact between them. "We should join the others before our absence is noticed," he said. He turned his back, walking to the door in a few long steps. But there he paused, resting his forehead on the wood. "It's just been a long time for me, since Noah. A long time since I *knew* a man I wanted to be with, Griffin. Knew him outside of a brothel or a club. It makes me worry, especially when you couple it with my fears of hurting Letty."

"I understand," Griffin said slowly. "I've never had a lover in Society. Nor one who was linked to my family. So it is fresh ground for both of us. And we'll both be mindful of it, we'll both work to make sure we aren't discovered."

"I hope so," Aaron whispered as he walked out into the hallway. "I hope so."

~

Aaron stood in the hallway, staring at the door to Griffin's room. It was after midnight and the house was quiet and still around him. Yet he didn't feel comfortable in what he was about to do. Once he did it, there would be no going back.

His heart raced as he lifted his hand for the third time and held a fist before the door.

"Do it or don't," he muttered to himself through clenched teeth.

Finally he forced his knuckles to brush the door, knocking

softly. When it didn't immediately open, he spun to walk away, but he hadn't made it a step when the door opened behind him.

"Where are you going?" Griffin's low voice asked, like a rope thrown out around Aaron's waist, drawing him back.

Slowly Aaron turned and faced him. His breath hitched. Griffin's jacket and cravat had long been discarded, leaving him in a half-unbuttoned shirt, trousers slung low around trim hips and no shoes or stockings. His hair was slightly mussed, almost bed-tossed, and it made Aaron want to shove his fingers into it and tug his mouth to Griffin's.

Instead, he cleared his throat. "I wasn't sure you were in."

Griffin arched a brow. "Well, I am. Join me."

Those two words were like a siren's song. With a sigh, Aaron followed it, walking past Griffin into his bedroom. He heard Griffin shut the door and then he caught Aaron's arm, pulling him back to flatten him against the barrier. Griffin's mouth crushed down on his and his tongue pierced through the thin line of his lips.

Aaron's mind emptied as he opened, arching into Griffin as his arms came around the other man's shoulders. Their mouths merged for a while as the air around them crackled with wild abandon and passionate surrender. Griffin's hands moved and Aaron didn't resist as he unbuttoned Aaron's jacket, untied his cravat, opened his shirt.

Griffin pulled back as he slipped all the layers above Aaron's waist away, and Aaron's stomach clenched at his wicked smile as Griffin looked him up and down. "Better than I dreamed," he growled.

"You too," Aaron agreed, opening Griffin's shirt in turn and shoving it aside. Griffin's skin was hot when Aaron touched it, smooth, and when he leaned down and pressed his mouth to Griffin's shoulder blade, he tasted as good as he smelled.

Griffin sucked air in through his teeth as Aaron nibbled lower, rolling his tongue over his nipple and loving how Griffin's body tensed in response. He wanted to learn every one of this man's pleasure points, he wanted to use them against Griffin until he was panting and begging for release. He wanted to play with him until he couldn't take it anymore.

It had been a long time since he felt such a powerful longing. In the brothels and the clubs, sex was a perfunctory action, a way to slake a desire. This was something different.

This was pulsing, driving need, and it felt like a wave that washed up over him and tugged him to the bottom of an endless ocean. He was helpless to it, he no longer had the strength to fight it. At least not right now.

He dropped to his knees and let his mouth move lower, flattening his tongue over Griffin's toned stomach muscles as he loosened the other man's trousers. A thick erection was already outlined in the rough fabric and Aaron held his breath as he peeled them away and revealed Griffin's cock. It was gorgeous. Griffin was tall and had a wiry strength, and his cock reflected that body type. Heavy and hard, but not too thick, not too long. Just perfect.

Aaron glanced up the naked length of Griffin's body, meeting the other man's eyes as he wrapped his mouth around him. Griffin let out a low moan, but didn't break the intense eye contact as Aaron began to suck him. He took him deep inside, almost all the way to the back of his throat, while he held tight to the base of Griffin's cock, gently stroking the length his mouth couldn't accommodate.

Griffin's pupils dilated as Aaron did his slow work, his pleasure obvious by his soft grunts, as well as by the way his cock swelled even bigger. Aaron took it all, reveling in the saltiness of Griffin's skin, the hard thrust of him filling Aaron's mouth, the way his hands moved into Aaron's hair and his fingers clenched against his scalp. He was going to make Griffin come, just as Griffin had made him come earlier in the day.

At least he thought he was going to do so. But just as he felt the shift in Griffin's reaction, the subtle movement toward release, Griffin pulled from his lips, grabbed his arms and tugged him to his feet. He cupped Aaron's backside, flattening his body to his, and kissed him deeply.

"I want to be inside of you," Griffin said when he pulled away. "Is that something you...*like*?"

Aaron swallowed hard, memories and emotions flooding him with unexpected power. He shrugged away from Griffin and took a step back as he tried to calm himself.

"What is it?" Griffin asked.

Aaron took a deep breath, forcing himself to keep looking at Griffin even though he wanted to turn away, to not reveal the vulnerability that screamed in his chest, in his mind.

"I-I do like that," he admitted softly. "But...but..."

Griffin stepped forward and reached out to take his hand. He threaded their fingers together and tugged Aaron a step closer as he lifted Aaron's hand to his heart. Aaron could feel the steady beat of it beneath Griffin's warm skin, and that rhythm soothed him a little.

"You can tell me," Griffin whispered.

"I haven't had a man inside of me since Noah died," Aaron admitted, heat flooding his cheeks at the confession.

Griffin's eyes widened. "But—but I saw you at the brothels and the clubs."

Aaron nodded. "Yes. But I only got sucked off there, and sucked off other men. I never did...the other. It felt too intimate to do with a stranger."

Griffin's lips pursed. "I understand." He lifted the hand on his chest to his lips and kissed it. "Aaron, if you don't want to do that, we can do so many other things. I wouldn't force you."

Aaron stared at him, feeling his kindness, his acceptance. It had been a long time since he felt so connected to a man. Since Noah. And he found he didn't want to just do the things he'd done with prostitutes and anonymous lovers. He wanted that deeper intimacy. He wanted something to remember when this party was over and Griffin was once again a distant star. Something to admire, but never dream of touching.

"I want you to," he murmured. "I want *you* to, Griffin."

A slow, broad smile spread over Griffin's handsome face. He

cupped Aaron's cheek and leaned in, kissing him deeply. Aaron lifted his arms around Griffin's neck and surrendered to that kiss. Tears stung his eyes as he did so, the power of this moment suddenly overwhelming.

Griffin slowly moved him backward across the room, to the high bed near the fireplace. When they'd reached it, Griffin pulled back and smiled at him.

"Will you remove the rest of your clothing while I get what I need to ready you?" he asked.

Aaron swallowed and nodded. "Yes."

Griffin kissed him one last, gentle time and then turned to leave the room for his attaching dressing area. Once he was gone, Aaron took a long breath. He removed his shoes, stockings and trousers, shivering as the air hit his overheated skin.

Griffin returned, a small bottle in his hand, and set it on the nightstand. Then he stepped back and looked Aaron up and down.

"I saw a little of you in the woods today," he drawled. "But this is so much better."

Aaron nodded. "I can't believe we're doing this."

Griffin met his eyes. "You've confessed something to me, Aaron, so I must confess something to you."

Aaron lifted both eyebrows in surprise. "Very well. What is your confession?"

"I've wanted to do this with you for a long time. After I saw you in one of the clubs for the first time, after I realized you were like… like me…I found myself dreaming of exactly this moment."

Aaron caught his breath. "That is a powerful statement."

"That isn't my confession, though. One night you went to one of the rooms at the Wild Boar that had…an observation area."

Aaron straightened slightly. "Yes?"

"I-I followed you," Griffin said softly. "I watched you."

Aaron's heart began to throb faster as he stared at Griffin. "You watched me."

Griffin nodded slowly. "You were with a prostitute. I watched you take him in your mouth. Watched him do the same for you."

He could see Griffin was nervous making this confession. Not that Aaron blamed him. He'd sometimes chosen the rooms where people could watch at the club, especially if his partner liked the idea, but it had always still felt anonymous to do so.

Knowing Griffin had been behind the false wall, watching him do something so intimate…it was incredibly arousing.

"And what did you do?" Aaron asked, moving toward him.

Griffin's pupils dilated further. His cock seemed to grow even harder, and Aaron clenched in need and anticipation. "I took myself in hand."

"Watching me fuck another man's mouth."

"Pretending it was mine," Griffin whispered, his voice impossibly rough and sensual. "I did the same thing so many times after. It became my favorite fantasy."

Aaron reached out, smoothing his hand over Griffin's cock. "And now we're here together tonight."

"And fantasy is about to be reality," Griffin groaned. "As long as you're not angry over what I did."

Aaron tugged him harder, smoothing his thumb over the swollen head of Griffin's cock and eliciting a harsh moan from him. "Do I seem angry?"

Griffin shook his head. "No."

With that, he leaned in and kissed Aaron once more. Aaron melted against him, surrendering to the gentle insistence of Griffin's mouth, of his naked body rubbing against Aaron's.

Aaron pulsed with need, but there was something more that clouded his desire-addled mind and made his hands and body shake. A thought that infected him.

He could love this man. Perhaps he already did love this man. And that was impossible. But this night wasn't. So he had to take it and then make sure it was the only time.

CHAPTER 5

As he leaned Aaron into the edge of the bed, Griffin felt a shift in their kiss. A desperation that made him smile. Aaron wanted him and was willing to allow Griffin the intimacy of taking him.

Griffin wasn't going to abuse that trust. He pulled away from the kiss with a shiver of desire. "Turn around," he said softly.

Aaron let out a great shudder before he followed the direction, clenching his fists against the bedclothes and bending at the waist to offer Griffin a gorgeous view of his tight ass. Griffin's mouth watered at the sight and his hands shook as he reached for the bottle of oil he'd set beside the bed. He took his time uncorking it, then raised it above Aaron and drizzled a little of the cold liquid down over his entrance.

Aaron sucked his breath in through his teeth and arched his back. Griffin smiled and reached down to brush just his fingertips across the crack of Aaron's ass. He teased, never quite touching the hole, just brushing around it until Aaron pushed back against him with an impatient grunt.

Griffin took in a breath. It had been a long time since Aaron had done this, so for both emotional and physical reasons Griffin had to go slowly. Even if he wanted to just take, he had to resist so this night would be incredible for both of them.

He pressed his index finger against the rosette of Aaron's backside and gently pushed, letting the tip dip inside to begin to coat the channel with oil.

"Oh God," Aaron moaned, burying his head against the coverlet as his fingers clenched into the fabric.

Griffin pressed farther, inserting his finger past the tightness of muscle into the warm welcome within. Aaron flexed around him, his body rippling and pulling Griffin even deeper inside. Griffin squeezed his eyes shut, so ready to feel that same pulse around his cock.

He pushed a second finger into the entrance, playing, pushing and finally penetrating so he could gently stretch Aaron and ready him for all to come.

"It's been…" Aaron gasped. "Such a long time."

Griffin leaned down and pressed a kiss to the smooth expanse of Aaron's back and the other man jolted, arching his hips and pulling Griffin farther inside. He took the unspoken hint, the wordless invitation of Aaron's body, and began to pump his two fingers back and forth, in and out. Aaron's cock twitched in time and he gasped in pleasure with every thrust.

Griffin let it go on like that for a while, but his own body was screaming with desire by now. He needed Aaron and he wasn't going to be able to wait much longer.

As if he could read Griffin's mind, Aaron looked at him over his shoulder. The two men locked eyes and Aaron gave him a soft smile.

"Do it," he whispered. "I want you to."

Griffin groaned at the invitation and slowly let his fingers slide from Aaron's ass. He stroked his cock with his slick hand, spreading more of the liquid across his length before he positioned himself behind Aaron. Aaron straightened slightly, tilting his hips to grant him access.

Griffin pressed the tip of his cock to Aaron's ass and pushed gently. There was a moment of exquisite resistance and then the ring gave way and he slid inside an inch. Both men grunted in time and Aaron's ass flexed, drawing Griffin inside.

Tight heat enveloped him as he slowly pulsed forward, better than a mouth, better than a fist. Better than anything. He reached around to cup Aaron's cock as he thrust all the way to the hilt at last. Aaron was rock hard, the tip of him slick with precum.

"Oh God," Aaron whimpered, thrusting against Griffin's hand.

He cupped Aaron, jerking at him. At first he was gentle, loving the stretch of Aaron's body, the heat that squeezed him so perfectly. But as his pleasure and his excitement grew, his thrusts grew harder, as did his jerks of Aaron's cock.

Their breathing quickened together, until they were both panting. Griffin's vision was beginning to blur, his legs were beginning to shake, and his balls tightened to his body in preparation for release.

It hit him like a volcano, sudden and explosive, and he thrust hard as his come filled Aaron. And as if that were permission, Aaron said his name and came along with him. They collapsed together over the edge of the bed, their hands entangling, their bodies still joined, the only sounds around them the matching raggedness of their breath.

Griffin didn't know how long they lay like that, tangled and sweaty on the edge of his bed, but at last he rolled to the side, his cock falling free of Aaron's body. He took a place on his bed and Aaron joined him, resting his head in the crook of Griffin's shoulder as they lay together.

"You told me you loved Noah," Griffin said, slowly tracing circles on Aaron's bare shoulder.

Aaron was silent for a long moment. Then he nodded. "I did. And he loved me."

"And was tonight…all right then? You don't regret letting me do what you had only shared with him?"

He held his breath as he waited for the answer, its importance clear to him. Aaron tilted his head and looked up at him.

"Yes," he said softly. "It was amazing." Griffin smiled in relief, but the smile fell when Aaron said, "And what of you? Have you ever loved?"

Griffin pressed his lips together hard. "I hated myself for being different. You remember when I got into all that trouble when Letty met Jack. I was trying to join Jack's criminal enterprise—I even went to his enemy and nearly got my sister and her husband killed in the process."

Aaron shuddered. "I remember that very well, yes. You did it because you were...?"

"Confused," Griffin whispered. "I didn't fit and I wanted to find a way to do so. Not the way my body told me I'd fit, but something else. But once Letty and Jack were nearly killed thanks to me, I knew I couldn't fight what I was anymore. Fighting it was as dangerous as accepting it. But I still didn't get up the gumption to go to a club and find a man who would have me for almost two years."

"And yet you did," Aaron said softly.

Griffin nodded. "At last, yes. It was such a relief *feeling* something, wanting something. But I swore it would only be physical for me. After all, my father and I had a strained enough relationship. I couldn't risk him having yet another thing to disapprove of, or worse yet, hate me for."

Aaron rolled and leaned up on his elbows until they were face to face. "So you only ever went to brothels and the anonymous clubs?"

Griffin sighed. "Yes."

Aaron's face was solemn. "It's complicated for men like us."

Griffin examined Aaron's face. He was so damned handsome. Griffin had always thought that, and always admired him for how he'd brought himself up in the world. But what he felt right now was more than mere attraction or esteem. He was beginning to realize he was falling in love with him.

"It doesn't have to be complicated," he said, reaching out to touch Aaron's face with the back of his hand.

Aaron's eyes widened as he leaned into Griffin's touch. "No?" he whispered.

Griffin sat up and cupped Aaron's cheeks, drawing him up his body for a kiss. But before their lips touched, he whispered, "No."

And then he was drowning in Aaron again, lost in desire and passion, need and love. And he'd never felt better.

Aaron picked up his jacket from the floor and quietly slipped it over his shoulders. He moved to the mirror, and in the dim light from the dying fire, he smoothed some of the wildness of his hair.

Then he turned back to the bed. Griffin was sleeping there, sprawled across the mattress, one bare leg kicked out from the covers. He had a slight smile on his face as he slept.

Aaron squeezed his eyes shut as a swell of emotion flooded him. He was in love with Griffin. It was true. Their night of unbridled passion had only solidified feelings he'd been trying to ignore since the first time he'd spied Griffin in a club.

Griffin had said their passion didn't have to be complicated. Was that true? After all, they both spent most of their time living in London. They could see each other there, under the guise of a friendship, and no one would know. If they were discreet, if they were careful of what the servants saw…

It *could* work. Letty wouldn't have to be hurt, no one would have to know and threaten their businesses or their lives. Aaron caught his breath at the power of that hope that blossomed inside of him. He hadn't felt it since Noah drew his last breath all those years before.

He turned to the door and crept into the hallway. He moved toward the guest wing of the house, but hadn't gotten more than a step when Jack strode out of his and Letty's bedroom, tightening a robe around his waist. The two men nearly collided with each other.

Aaron froze in terror as Jack's face registered surprise at his unexpected appearance.

"Aaron?" Jack whispered, tugging the bedroom door shut behind him and moving toward him. "What are you doing up so early?"

Aaron could hardly breathe as he stared at Jack. "I-I-I was having a hard time sleeping," he gasped out. "I thought I might go for a walk around the estate to calm my mind."

Jack slowly looked down the long hallway toward the guest quarters and then back to Aaron. Panic gripped Aaron. He could read Jack's questions on his face. Why was Aaron in the hall of the family quarters, why was he standing outside Griffin's door and, if Jack was observant, why was Aaron still wearing his clothing from last night?

Why, why, why…

"Why are *you* up so early?" Aaron blurted out, hearing the defensiveness in his voice.

Jack smiled and tossed a look back toward the room. "I know Leticia hasn't said anything, but she won't mind if I tell you. She's pregnant again. Sometimes in the middle of the night she gets a wild notion that she wants sausage or roast or…" He shuddered. "…brined vegetables. I try to indulge her as much I can."

Aaron's lips parted. "Pregnant? Congratulations."

He said the words and he meant them wholeheartedly, but even through his joy for Letty, he also felt horror and pain. He'd nearly been caught in an unexplainable situation. Even now, Jack might casually mention seeing Aaron in the hall and Letty could easily put the facts together.

In her delicate condition, God knew how she would react if she realized what was happening between Griffin and himself.

"Well, I'll leave you to your walk," Jack said, patting Aaron on the arm gently. "Good…morning, I suppose it's morning now."

Aaron nodded as he watched Jack walk away. Once he was gone, Aaron leaned against the wall for a moment, drawing short breaths that did nothing to calm him.

He'd allowed himself to hope for happiness of some kind with Griffin, but he could see now what a fantasy that was. Letty and Jack knew what Aaron wanted. If they saw Griffin and Aaron growing close, it wouldn't take much for them to put two and two together.

He would break Letty's heart once again. He didn't want to do that. Not ever again. So this was impossible. A dream, a fantasy.

No matter how much he cared for Griffin, he could *never* let last night happen again. And he could never let himself believe that they could have anything more than a few stolen kisses and a night of unforgettable passion.

He pushed away from the wall and trudged toward his chamber. He didn't want to sleep now, but he needed to make his bed look used, make his lies look real. He needed to think.

And to mourn the love he'd allowed himself to want and then lost before it could even begin.

Griffin couldn't stop smiling as he strode down the hall toward the breakfast room late the next morning. Despite very little sleep the night before, he felt exuberant, more than ready to face the day. And it was all thanks to Aaron.

They had shared something precious in those hours in his bed. Something he'd never let himself want or expect he would find. Now it was here and he embraced it wholeheartedly. They would work out the details, he was certain. They would make it work and never let anyone be hurt by the truth.

He stepped into the room and said a few welcomes to the guests around him. He scanned the table, and his smile widened as he found Aaron already seated. There was an empty place beside him and Griffin moved toward it. But as he grew near, Aaron looked up and his expression twisted not in welcome, but in rejection.

"Good morning," Griffin said, now a little more cautious in the face of the unexpected tension that all but pulsed through Aaron's being. When he'd awoken alone, he hadn't read much into it. After all, they couldn't exactly be caught together. He'd believed Aaron's silent retreat had been a kindness to let him sleep.

Now he had to wonder if there were much more to the wordless escape and cold bed Griffin had been left to.

Aaron cast him a side glance. "Morning," he muttered, and it sounded like the word was forced through clenched teeth.

Griffin took his place as a maid poured him tea. "May I get you anything, sir?" she asked.

He shook his head. "This is fine, thank you."

Once the girl had slipped away, Griffin returned his attention to Aaron. "What's wrong?" he asked softly.

Aaron shot him another side glance. "Nothing," he ground out, then pushed to his feet. "I think I'll take a walk this morning," he said louder, so the room would hear. "If you don't mind, Letty."

Letty glanced down the table, a look of surprise on her face. "No, of course not. It's a beautiful morning."

Griffin stared. Aaron was walking away? So determined to escape that he'd stride from the room in the middle of breakfast?

It seemed so, for Aaron tipped his head at the table at large and then walked from the room without a backward glance or acknowledgment for Griffin.

"Odd fellow, isn't it?" said one of the gentlemen on Griffin's other side.

Griffin cleared his throat and pushed his hurt aside. "I wouldn't say that," he said, his voice strained. "I have never been much for parties myself—having a moment alone is sometimes refreshing."

"Suppose," Griffin's companion grunted, and went back to shoveling eggs into his mouth.

Griffin leaned back in his chair and gazed at the door where

Aaron had just departed. He tried to keep his mind off Aaron, but he couldn't. He wanted to know what had changed him from Griffin's passionate lover to a man who couldn't even look Griffin in the face.

He got up and glanced at Letty and Jack. "I find I have a bit of a headache. I think I'll retire for a while if you don't mind."

Letty arched a brow. "Certainly, if you aren't well. We'll be playing pall-mall on the lawn at the big house later. Perhaps you'll join us."

Griffin nodded absentmindedly and then made his way out of the room. But he didn't go to his chamber. Instead, he walked out of the house and down the path that led to the lake. He had a feeling he would find Aaron there, just as they had found each other there the day they had arrived for the party.

He weaved his way over the rolling hills, trying to calm himself. The last thing he wanted to do was let his emotions take over and make whatever was happening here worse than it already was.

He came over the last hill and stopped. Aaron was sitting on the grass beside the water, his legs drawn up, his arms draped over them. He was staring off into the distance, his expression dark and pensive.

"Why did you leave?" Griffin called out as he came down the hill.

Aaron tensed before he looked over his shoulder. "Bloody hell, Griffin, why are you following me?"

"Because I thought everything was fine and then you…you…you wouldn't even look at me at breakfast." Griffin folded his arms. "And you left the room rather than even exchange pleasantries with me."

Slowly Aaron pushed to his feet and Griffin tensed. Even was he was upset, he appreciated the slow unfolding of Aaron's lean body. A body he now knew very well.

"What did you want me to do, Griffin, put my arms around you in the middle of the breakfast room?" Aaron's tone was harsh, and Griffin flinched.

"Of course not. But neither did I expect you to hardly look at me. Did I do something wrong? Is that why you snuck out of my bed this morning like a thief?"

Aaron took a step toward him. "Of course not. Look, you and I had a bit of fun last night. That was all. It's over now."

Griffin caught his breath at the sharp, dismissive words. He stared at Aaron, whose face was drawn and cold, hardly an expression on it. He seemed entirely disinterested, despite everything they had shared.

"Why?" Griffin asked. This time he was the one whose teeth were clenched.

Aaron shifted slightly. "I-I don't want you."

"I don't believe that."

Griffin moved toward him and caught Aaron's arms, dragging him forward. He slammed his mouth to Aaron's, driving his tongue inside and eliciting a needy moan from him. Aaron's arms came around him, molding their bodies together. He felt Aaron's cock harden, but more telling, he felt his pulse quicken. It fluttered beneath his skin, setting a hard rhythm that proved he was lying.

Griffin drew away, releasing Aaron, who spun away, staggering toward the lake a few steps as he drew in harsh breaths.

"You and I have been dancing around each other for months," Griffin growled. "Maybe even years. Every time I saw you at a club and our eyes met, we both recognized what we wanted in each other. Only here have we been unable to deny it, because it goes deeper than a fuck, and *you* know it. So what are you afraid of? And don't tell me Letty, because I know it's more than that."

Aaron lifted his chin. "I'm not afraid of anything."

Griffin shook his head. "Bollocks. If you won't say it, then I will. You're afraid of connecting again. Afraid of risking something more than your pleasure. And I understand that."

Aaron moved on him, his eyes flashing with anger and pain. "No, you don't. You're young, you don't have a clue what it's like to lose what you could never fully claim."

"I'd *love* to know," Griffin whispered, his pain pulsing through him in a dull, constant thud. "I've been alone my whole life and it's horrible. Never caring for anyone or having anyone care for you in return is an empty life. I don't want it anymore."

"Don't do this," Aaron said, scrubbing a hand over his face.

"I must," Griffin insisted. "Bloody hell, Aaron, you must know that I care for you. I more than merely care. I want that connection you've described. I want love."

Aaron shook his head slowly, and once again he wouldn't meet Griffin's eyes. "Well, I'm not the one."

Griffin swallowed hard, barely managing past the lump in his throat. "You may be the only one."

Aaron lifted his gaze, and in that moment Griffin saw all the love, all the fear, all the pain inside him. And he knew that Aaron would walk away, regardless of what his heart wanted. Maybe *because* of what it wanted.

And his own heart broke.

"I'm sorry," Aaron muttered, then turned and walked away for a second time that morning. Only this time, Griffin let him go.

This time, he recognized that there was nothing he could do to stop him.

CHAPTER 6

Griffin sat in the window seat in one of the parlors, looking out at the rainy afternoon. There was the soft click of the door shutting and he turned to find Letty standing at the entrance, leaning against the barrier as she watched him.

"Weren't you hosting whist or some such thing?" Griffin asked.

"Yes, it's a riotous game, I assure you," she said with a wide smile.

He tried to return it as best he could. "Mama is enjoying herself."

"She is. But there were enough players, so I thought I'd come look for *you*," Letty said, crossing the room to him at last and reaching out to take his hand. "You have not been yourself for two days, Griffin."

Griffin pursed his lips and turned his face so she wouldn't see his pain. Two days. Well, that marked the time exactly. Two days ago he'd been standing at the lake's edge with Aaron, his feelings rejected. And while he understood Aaron's reasons, the result stung no less.

"Perhaps I'm catching some affliction. I've heard told illness is common at gatherings," he said.

She sat down next to him. "It's more than that and I know it. Won't you talk to me?"

Griffin hesitated for a moment, then shook his head. "There is nothing to say, nor anything you can do for me. I just need…need…"

"What?" she encouraged him when he trailed off.

"I need to leave," he whispered.

She drew back, her eyes widening. "What?"

He nodded slowly. He'd been thinking of this very thing for a while now. Once it had been said out loud, his path was very clear. Going back to London, not being forced to look Aaron in the face every day—that was the best thing to overcome this pain.

"I don't want to ruin your gathering and I don't think I can muster any pleasure in it, Letty. But I came with Mama, and I don't want to—"

Letty lifted a hand. "Jack and War would be happy to provide you with a mount if you must leave, and one of the Woodley cousins would likely happily ride in the carriage with Mama back to London if you were to depart. *That* isn't my concern. Why do you feel you must go?"

He sighed. He would never tell her the whole truth, especially now that he was aware of what she'd gone through with her late husband. But he did say, "I just don't belong here, Letty."

Her lips pursed and she cleared her throat. "Aaron has also been acting oddly in the past few days. Did you two have a row?"

Griffin tensed. Here he had been thinking only of his own pain in Aaron's rejection, but now Letty's words focused him. Aaron had been afraid that she would find out and be hurt by any relationship between them. He'd told Griffin over and over that Letty would see if they weren't careful, that Letty would know.

And here she was, staring Griffin right in the eye, and it seemed Aaron's predictions were coming true. His feelings for Aaron were superseded by brotherly love as he shook his head.

"Mr. Condit and I don't know each other well enough for a row," he said, trying to make his tone distant, disinterested.

Letty arched a brow. "No? It seemed like you were becoming… friends."

Griffin pushed to his feet. "Well, we weren't," he said. "Now, you mentioned that War and Jack might give me a mount. Should I speak to them about it?"

Letty got to her feet slowly, and for a moment Griffin thought she might push him on the matter of Aaron. But finally, she nodded. "Yes. Neither of them is playing cards. They're in the stables, actually—there's a mare giving birth. But they say it's going smoothly, so I'm certain one of them can discuss it with you."

Griffin leaned forward to kiss her cheek. "I do appreciate your concern," he said. "And I promise that I'm…I'm very well."

He turned before she could answer, but he felt her stare on his back as he walked from the room, determined to leave not just to spare his own heart, but to protect her from a truth she should never have to face again.

Aaron leaned back as he watched the others play whist. He'd been asked to join a hand several times, but he knew he didn't have the focus in him at present. His thoughts were too mired by images of Griffin. Not just his kiss or his body joining with Aaron's, but of the pain on his face when Aaron had walked away from the love he offered.

He hated himself for doing it. And he could only hope that one day Griffin would understand there was no other answer.

A servant stepped into the room and looked around. When his gaze found Aaron, he moved forward. Leaning down, he said softly, "Mrs. Blackwood requests your company in the South Parlor."

Aaron glanced up at him in confusion. He'd actually thought Letty was still at the game, but now that he looked around, he noticed she wasn't anymore. So much for observation skills. One more reason he had to get Griffin out of his head.

"Thank you," he said, rising to his feet and slipping past the others as they played.

He made his way through the halls to the parlor and stepped inside to find Letty standing by the fire, hands folded in front of stomach, waiting for him.

"Would you have tea with me?" she asked, motioning to the set that had been placed on the sideboard.

He wrinkled his brow. After the game of whist was over, it had been made clear that the group as a whole would go up to the main house for tea.

"Of course," he said slowly, not fully understanding what Letty was doing, but unwilling to refuse her. They didn't often get to spend time together anymore.

She smiled as she waved him to a seat on the settee and began to pour. "I love having you here, you know."

He forced a smile to his own face. "It's always wonderful to see your family," he said, and in that he didn't have to lie. "After what you endured, you deserve everything good, Letty."

She handed him a cup and sat down across from him. "All that seems a lifetime ago. And sometimes it seems like it happened just in the span of a blink of an eye." She shook her head. "When I met Jack, I had all but given up on my happiness. Because of the...the *situation* with Noah, I thought I could never wed or else my virginity, despite being a widow, would reveal his secrets."

"I'm sorry," Aaron said, his voice cracking as he thought of those dark times. And of how he had betrayed her once more just a few days past.

She shook her head. "I'm not. Gracious, Aaron, at some point you must stop flagellating yourself for what happened with Noah. We all had good intentions, we all tried our best. The path we're on now is a result of what happened back then. Without your relationship with Noah, without what happened to our marriage, I might never have met Jack, nor married him and had our children. My life would be infinitely emptier. And Jack might have died in the life he was leading and that would be a great loss to this world."

Aaron nodded slowly. "I suppose I'd never considered it that way."

"The only regret I have is that I've never seen you find the same happiness that I have. At first I knew it was because you loved Noah. Losing him was devastating. But as the years passed, I kept waiting and hoping that I would sense you had fallen in love again. When you didn't, it was the only little blemish on my own happiness."

Aaron gritted his teeth. "Well, as we talked about before, it's more complicated for me."

"Of course it is. I just don't want you to make those complications even worse."

"What does that mean?" Aaron asked, his hand tightening in his lap.

Before she could answer, Griffin strode into the parlor. He was talking as he walked, "You were right that Jack and War were happy to loan me a horse. Hell, Jack wants to *give* me a horse, but you must convince him I'll pay because his mounts are worth a pretty penny. But since it's so late I won't leave until tomorr—"

He cut himself off as he realized Letty wasn't alone. Slowly Aaron got to his feet, trying to keep his pain at seeing Griffin from his face. It didn't matter how many times he did, whenever he faced him, it was like being stabbed in the broken heart.

"My apologies," Griffin said, his tone going cool and neutral. "When you asked me to join you, I assumed we would be alone. Good afternoon, Mr. Condit."

Aaron turned to Letty. "You asked your brother to join us?"

"I did. Griffin is going to leave us tomorrow morning and I wanted to talk to both of you before he did that." She looked at her brother. "Griffin, shut the door, will you?"

Aaron stared at Griffin, who met his eyes. The same terror was in his expression as Aaron felt in his own. Did Letty know? Was it their long disappearance during the scavenger hunt that had given them away, or had Jack told her he'd found Aaron outside Griffin's door? Or perhaps it was merely a look they'd exchanged.

Aaron's heart was racing as Griffin leaned back and slowly did as his sister asked.

"Sit beside Aaron on the settee, will you?" she said softly, an order disguised as a question.

Griffin looked like he was going to the gallows as he walked across the room and the men sat down together on the settee. Griffin's knee bumped his and Aaron felt electric awareness shoot through him.

"I'm going to speak plainly because I have a feeling you two have convinced yourselves that you are not allowed to do the same. Obviously, I know of Aaron's predilections. Am I right to know that you're now aware of our shared past with Noah, Griffin?"

Griffin leaned forward and caught her hands. "I *didn't* know until very recently, Letty. I'm so very sorry you went through such a difficult time. I had no idea."

Letty's face went soft and kind. "Oh Griffin, it was a long time ago. And yes, it was painful, but I was just explaining to Aaron that the pain had a purpose. And it placed me where I am, which is exactly where I want to be. So I don't look back at that time with anguish, but with love for Noah and for Aaron, as well as gratitude that I have the life I have today."

Griffin squeezed her hands. "You are so good, so forgiving."

She shrugged off the compliment. "What you might not know is that I am also aware of *your* desires, Griffin."

All the color drained from Griffin's face, and he looked so stricken that Aaron wanted to wrap his arms around him and draw him close for comfort. But he couldn't, of course he couldn't.

"I-I don't know what you mean," Griffin croaked, pulling his hands away.

She leaned back, a look of incredulity on her face. "Oh darling, I didn't guess it back when you had your difficulties with Jack, but over time I recognized your acting out, your feeling like you didn't fit…as what it was. I saw a great many signs and suddenly every-thing became clear."

"Letty," Griffin whispered.

Letty reached across the gap and took his hand once more. Aaron squeezed his eyes shut as the tingle of tears filled them. How often had she done the same for him, accepting him and loving him without hesitation or limitation? That kind of kindness and love was so rare—it was why he so wanted to protect her.

"I long ago came to believe that how you feel isn't some kind of choice you've made out of spite," she said. "And if you were created this way, there is no mistake to it. Whatever Society would say or do to you because of who and what you are, *I* don't judge it. Of course, at first I was afraid. The laws…the consequences…they are grave. But so are the consequences of locking away love from your life. I want you to be happy."

"Well, it's complicated," Griffin began.

Letty interrupted him with a bark of laughter. "There's that word again. You parrot each other so beautifully, it is no wonder I see you together."

Aaron jolted as both he and Griffin said, "What?" at the same time.

Her smile grew wider at the shared outburst, and she nodded. "I've seen you interact in passing and a little idea came to my mind. I decided to bring you both here in the hopes I could orchestrate some kind of romance."

Griffin stared at her, his mouth dropped open in silent shock. Aaron could barely catch his breath, but he managed to choke out, "You—you played *matchmaker?*"

"I intended to do so. I suppose I still *did*. After all I, ensured you were matched together for the scavenger hunt and placed you next to each other when I could," she said.

Griffin's eyes went even wider. "You manipulated the scavenger hunt?" he said with a shake of his head.

"Yes," she admitted freely and without a hint of apology. "You two even had clues different from everyone else's so you could spend time together. Oh, they ended in the correct place, of course —you *could* have won. But that wasn't the prize I hoped you'd find."

"I didn't think you had it in you," Aaron breathed.

She laughed. "You will find being married to a once-notorious criminal gives one a bit more willingness to cheat to get what one wants. Only I realized quite quickly that my machinations were not really effective. After all, almost immediately upon seeing you together I realized there was already a tension between you. I was only adding fuel to a fire, not setting the foundation for it."

"Do you think the others saw the same thing?" Aaron whispered, bile rising in his chest.

"No, of course not. I was looking for signs you two had a connection. More than half the ladies don't even realize such a thing could exist between men. The men know, but they don't look for it. Though when it comes to our scandalous family, I honestly doubt the Woodleys would even blink about it."

Griffin dipped his head. "There are different levels of scandal, Letty. And you know it."

Her expression softened. "Very well, you're right. As I said, I am not blind to the dangers."

"And not just the legal ones. What about Mama? She wants me to marry. She devotes a great deal of time in London to encouraging me to do so. What would she think about this, even if it could be?"

Letty nodded. "Yes, I've been pondering that. Mama is very happy here, you know. She loves being around Aunt Susanna and Mr. Gray. And she adores being near the children. Aunt Susanna has expressed an openness to asking her to stay here in the big house indefinitely. If she had a focus on her grandchildren, she would not be so focused on you. And I would do everything in my power to calm her drive to force you into something you didn't want. Without revealing your secret, of course."

Griffin blinked. "You would?"

"Yes. But these are all details and that *isn't* the point of what I'm saying to you both. The point is that I want you two to be happy. And if you could be happy together, that would be even better for me. I already know Aaron and trust him, so I wouldn't worry about who he was or what his motives were with you, Griffin. And Aaron, I also know how capable my brother is of great love and loyalty, which is no less than you deserve."

Aaron had listened to all she said, and now he got to his feet. His hands were shaking and he stared down at her, almost feeling like he was looking at a stranger, not his best friend of many, many years.

"Could you truly want this?" he asked, now daring to look at Griffin from the corner of his eye. His heart swelled when he did so. "After what I did to you in the past, you would offer me this?"

Now Letty stood. "I would never be so cruel as to deny two people I adore a happy future. So if fears about me, if guilt about the past, was stopping you, if it caused the friction between you that makes Griffin want to leave…I free you from it."

Aaron nearly buckled at the weight she lifted from his shoulders. With a gasp, he turned to look at Griffin and found him staring up at him. There was hope in his eyes. And for the first time, Aaron felt the full joy of hope in his own heart.

Letty released his hands and let out a long sigh. "Well, now that *that* has been said, I have a favor to ask of you both."

"What is it?" Griffin asked, getting to his feet.

"I left my cloak in the old caretaker cottage that is on the path to the main house. I must go rally everyone to head up there for tea now, but would you two mind taking the path ahead of us and fetching it?"

Griffin's brow wrinkled. "You need *us* to do that?" he asked.

She smiled as she leaned in to kiss first her brother's cheek, then Aaron's. "Quite desperately. Though to be honest, I don't need the item in any hurry. So go fetch it, but don't feel a strong need to rush up to the main house. I'll make an excuse for you."

She was grinning as she left the room, leaving Aaron and Griffin alone. They turned to face each other, staring for what seemed to be an eternity. Then Griffin cleared his throat.

"I-I suppose we should do as she asks," he said. "We can talk more freely at the cottage at any rate."

Aaron nodded. "Very well. Lead the way."

Griffin swallowed hard and motioned for the door and they left the parlor together to go to the cottage. But as they exited the house and started up the path, Aaron couldn't help but feel they were starting a new chapter together.

He could only hope it would be a chapter with a happy ending. Because until they could remove the walls between them, happiness was not a given.

CHAPTER 7

Griffin pressed open the door to the old caretaker's cottage, expecting to find it dark and dusty. After all, no one had lived here since his cousin Audrey's husband Jude still worked for Edward. But as he stepped inside, he caught his breath. The open room in the front was clean and quiet, except for a crackling fire that had been laid there. There was a basket on the table by the window with what looked to be food and wine.

Aaron looked around in wonder. "It's lovely."

Griffin nodded as he shut the door and latched it. "I have a feeling this is the Woodley tryst cottage. And now Letty has sent us here to look for her 'cloak'. With a fire burning and food set out."

Aaron slowly faced him, his expression unreadable. "And should we look for it?"

"There is no cloak, and I think that's clear to us both now," Griffin whispered. "She sent us here because…because…"

"Because she set us free," Aaron said softly.

Griffin wrinkled his brow. "*Are* you free, Aaron? Yes, fears of Letty's reaction were part of our shared hesitations about this thing between us, but it is more than that. *You* are afraid of love."

Aaron scrubbed a hand over his face. "I'm not afraid of love. I'm

—I'm afraid of losing love. You were right about that. I'd told myself I'd never love again, but once I fell in love with you it terrified me and—"

Griffin caught his breath and stepped forward. "Did you just say you loved me?" he interrupted.

Aaron blinked, and then understanding dawned. "Yes, I suppose I did." Now he moved forward. "And it is true, Griffin. I am in love with you."

Griffin shut his eyes as pure joy moved through him. Before he could open them, he felt Aaron's mouth on his in a kiss. He moaned at the brush of his lips and wrapped his arms around Aaron, dragging him closer as he opened to the man, welcoming him inside in every way.

The kiss was passionate and wild, free in a way they'd never been before. Their union had been blessed by the only person who mattered, and everything else could be worked out after…after…

Griffin pulled away from the kiss and took Aaron's hand. Wordlessly, he drew him into the bedroom in the back of the cottage. He shut the door and they stared at the bed together.

"There won't be any oil to ease the way," Griffin whispered, his voice gruff with the need that now boiled in him.

Aaron turned and began to unloop Griffin's cravat. "Oh, but there will be pleasure," he promised.

Griffin smiled and unbuttoned Aaron's coat. They undressed each other, mouths brushing skin, hands touching, eyes locked. By the time he was naked, Griffin was all but vibrating with need and his cock was hard as stone against his belly, just as Aaron's was.

Aaron took his hand and led him to the bed. There was a wickedness to his expression that Griffin had never seen before, an ease that filled his heart with as much pleasure as Aaron's body did.

Aaron pushed him back onto the bed and then crawled up to join him. He kissed Griffin deeply, his hands smoothing over Griffin's body, then he shifted position. He crawled so that his head was at Griffin's cock and his cock at Griffin's head.

Griffin smiled. He saw what Aaron wanted to do. He rolled toward him, giving him better access as he reached out to catch Aaron's hard cock in his fist. He guided Aaron to his mouth and slowly slid his tongue around the head.

Aaron let out a moan, then Griffin's cock was being pulled into hot, wet heaven and Aaron's tongue stroked him in much the same way. It was pleasure for pleasure now, a slow race to completion. He tried to remain focused on the hard cock inside his mouth, on the man who he loved and wanted to give so much pleasure to. It was almost impossible when Aaron was swirling his tongue over Griffin's length and taking him deep into his throat until Griffin's vision blurred.

He sucked harder, a challenge to Aaron's resolve. And it worked. Aaron began to moan against his cock, flexing his hips in time to the strokes of Griffin's mouth. The vibration of the sound shot through Griffin's cock, and his balls tightened as his pleasure grew.

He was going to come and he wanted Aaron there with him. He increased his pace, Aaron matched it, over and over they moved, and finally Griffin grunted as he came in long, heavy thrusts just in the same moment as Aaron's salty essence filled his mouth.

He took every drop, reveling in this part of his lover he had now claimed, in the part of himself he had shared. It was a sacred exchange, as important to him as any vow they could make.

He panted as he let Aaron's cock pop free from his mouth. Slowly Aaron did the same, and turned to crawl up the bed and sprawl into Griffin's arms. They lay like that for what felt like a blissful eternity. Griffin traced the lines of Aaron's back with his fingertips, memorizing each flexing muscle, each warm inch.

Finally, he leaned back so he could look more closely at Aaron's face. "You know I love you, too, don't you?"

Aaron smiled. "I hoped, but wasn't certain. Do you? *Could* you? Could I be so lucky twice?"

Griffin leaned forward, kissing him, tasting the merging flavors of their bodies that was infinitely erotic and wonderful. "We are both lucky."

Aaron sighed as he settled back against Griffin's chest. "But what do we do now? Letty has approved, but Society is still dangerous. What is your plan?"

Griffin stared at the ceiling above him as he pondered that question. "A few days ago, I made clear to you the complications my father created in my inheritance. I was not only using that as a ploy to get near you. It is true—I need more than a mere solicitor. A man of affairs would be useful beyond measure."

Aaron leaned up. "And you want me to be your man of *affairs*?"

Griffin laughed, lighter than he'd been in ages. "Most definitely. No one would blink an eye at the appointment. The world knows how talented in finance and legalities you are. And that you would certainly come highly recommended by my sister. Many men of that profession live in the same home as their employer, and they spend a great deal of time together. It would offer us some protection against the laws. And outside of my home and any club we attend together, we would be very careful."

Aaron nodded. He knew of other men who had the same kind of arrangements with their lovers. "And would you insist that I not work with others?"

Griffin arched a brow. "Are you asking if I would make you a kept man?"

"I want to truly be your partner, Griffin, not someone you pay to fuck. So if you hire me, our work together must be real. And I would like to continue with a few of my clients. I've worked hard to build my reputation."

Griffin sat up. "I would never take away anything you've built, Aaron. You would truly be my partner, as well as my lover. And I would be luckier to have you than you will be to have me. What say you?"

Aaron stared up at him for a long moment before he, too, sat up. He reached out to cup Griffin's cheek, drawing him closer.

"I would say that we are both lucky. And that I love you. And that I would be happy to become your man of affairs. In your life and your bed. As long as you'll have me."

"That would be forever," Griffin growled as he brushed his lips against Aaron's.

"Forever sounds perfect to me," Aaron whispered in return, and then passion took over, a celebration of their love and their future to come.

READ AN EXCERPT OF THE DARING DUKE

He ignored the statement as they turned through the crowd. "You were a great help with the…situation with my mother tonight," he said softly.

Her lips parted again in surprise and he had a flash of a moment where he wondered what they would taste like. He shook his head again to clear his mind. Damn, but he was rattled by his mother's actions.

"Everyone gets overheated from time to time at a ball," Miss Liston said carefully. "I was happy to be of assistance. I hope she is feeling better."

"She is going home," he said. "And we both know she wasn't merely overheated."

She swallowed hard and looked up to meet his gaze. Once again he was struck by how stunning her eyes were. He didn't think he'd ever seen such a combination of blue and green before.

"If anyone asked me," she said slowly, "that would be what I would tell them. It is all I recall, at any rate."

He wrinkled his brow at her reassurance, kindly made and

somehow unexpected. "If you said something else, it might bring you a little renown."

Her eyes narrowed. "Please don't presume you know me well enough to believe I would trade renown for someone else's reputation, Your Grace. I didn't help your sister or your mother in order to gain something from the act. There is decency without price in this world. If you do not know that, I am sorry for you."

James arched a brow at her heated response. When she was emotional, she was far more animated and a blush crept into her cheeks and down her neck, disappearing into the bust of her gown.

"I apologize, Miss Liston," he said, inclining his head. "I did not mean to imply that you would be mercenary. Truly."

Her expression softened a touch. "I'm sure there are some who might be. I'm simply not one of them."

"Then we are lucky you were the friend my sister was with," he said. "And once again, I thank you."

"Your sister is lovely," Miss Liston said, looking over his shoulder into the crowd of other dancers.

When he turned her, he saw that Meg was dancing with Simon. She was smiling and laughing, and his heart got lighter seeing it.

"She is, indeed," he said. "She likes you."

The music had begun to slow and Miss Liston looked up at him with wide eyes. "Does she? I cannot imagine why. We do not have anything in common."

He laughed at her candor, even if he didn't believe her words. "You are both clever. And clearly you are both kind. That is the foundation of many a friendship, Miss Liston."

The music stopped and he bowed to her, then offered her a hand to escort her from the floor. When they reached the edge, he swept the cloak of his personality around him and said, "It was a great pleasure to dance with you, Miss Liston. I hope you will allow me the pleasure again."

To his surprise, she didn't titter as other women might have. Instead, she folded her arms across her chest like a shield and pressed those surprisingly full lips together until they were a tight line.

"Your Grace, we both know this was a pity dance, thrown at me as some kind of reward for my help. And clearly it was also a way to determine if I would use whatever I saw tonight against you. Please don't pretend it was something more. I understand the way the world works."

He drew back. "You are direct."

Panic flooded her face and she shifted with discomfort. "Well, a woman of my position must be practical and not allow herself to get swept away by foolish notions."

"Like that I could have actually enjoyed dancing with you?" he asked with a slight smile. "It is so hard for you to believe."

She shrugged. "I'm not exactly in your sphere, Your Grace."

"Miss Liston, whether you believe it or not, I did truly enjoy my time with you," he said, and was surprised to find he actually meant those words. Normally when he danced with ladies, he went through the motions, trying to be polite while he awaited escape. This dance had been different. Emma Liston was…interesting.

She bent her head. "Well, I…I…thank you. Now I should go find my mother. Good night, Your Grace."

He inclined his head. "Good night, Emma."

She stiffened at the use of her given name, but she didn't correct him before she turned away and rushed off through the crowd, leaving James alone to watch her. And watch her he did, until she vanished into the crowd and left him entirely confused by their encounter.

ALSO BY JESS MICHAELS

Theirs

Their Marchioness

Their Duchess

Their Countess

Their Bride

The Kent's Row Duchesses

No Dukes Allowed

Not Another Duke

Not the Duke You Marry

Regency Royals

To Protect a Princess

Earl's Choice

Princes are Wild

To Kiss a King

The Queen's Man

The Three Mrs

The Unexpected Wife

The Defiant Wife

The Duke's Wife

The Duke's By-Blows

The Love of a Libertine

The Heart of a Hellion

The Matter of a Marquess

The Redemption of a Rogue

The 1797 Club

The Daring Duke

Her Favorite Duke

The Broken Duke

The Silent Duke

The Duke of Nothing

The Undercover Duke

The Duke of Hearts

The Duke Who Lied

The Duke of Desire

The Last Duke

The Scandal Sheet

The Return of Lady Jane

Stealing the Duke

Lady No Says Yes

My Fair Viscount

Guarding the Countess

The House of Pleasure

Seasons

An Affair in Winter

A Spring Deception

One Summer of Surrender

Adored in Autumn

The Wicked Woodleys

Forbidden

Deceived

Tempted

Ruined

Seduced

Fascinated

To see a complete listing of Jess Michaels' titles, please visit:

http://www.authorjessmichaels.com/books

ABOUT THE AUTHOR

USA Today Bestselling author Jess Michaels likes geeky stuff, Cherry Vanilla Coke Zero, anything coconut, cheese and her dog, Elton. She is lucky enough to be married to her favorite person in the world and lives in Oregon settled between the ocean and the mountains.

When she's not trying out new flavors of Greek yogurt or rewatching Bob's Burgers over and over and over (she's a Tina), she writes historical romances with smoking hot characters and emotional stories. She has written for numerous publishers and is now fully indie and loving every moment of it (well, almost every moment).

Jess loves to hear from fans! So please feel free to contact her at Jess@AuthorJessMichaels.com.

Jess Michaels offers a free book to members of her newsletter, so sign up on her website:
http://www.AuthorJessMichaels.com/

facebook.com/JessMichaelsBks
instagram.com/JessMichaelsBks
bookbub.com/authors/jess-michaels

9 781958 358139